Silk & Bones

Book One

Sin's Bastards Mc Series

Credits

K.J. Dahlen
Silk & Bones
Sin's Bastards Mc Series
Copyright © 2018
Book Design & Formatting: Wicked Muse[1]
Cover Art Provided By Talia's Book Covers[2]

---

1. https://www.facebook.com/bonnie.l.elliott.7/

2. https://www.facebook.com/Taliasbookcovers/

Dedication

To: Dave, Tessie and Dave, Steve and Julie, Heather and Jamey, DJ and Jess, Brittney and Jay, Ron and Judy, Dawn and Tim, Chele and Andy, & Robin- friends and family, the two things in life that matter the most.

Thank you Leanore – you made my dream possible.

Prologue

Melora blew the smoke out of her mouth and sighed. It was long after midnight and she was taking a short break. The noise from the bar was muted behind her but she could still hear the hum of people and music. The shadows of the night and the dumpster Melora was hiding behind hid her from the populace but she didn't care. She gazed down at the dirty alley she was in and suppressed a grimace. She should be used to this sort of place but it didn't mean she didn't want something better.

Sighing, she scratched an itch under her wig and pushed the hairpiece back into place. The long dark brown hairpiece hid her real hair and had since she'd gotten to town. She wore several wigs over the time she'd been here, all different colors. Some days, she was blonde and others she wore a red wig. For the last few weeks, she'd worn a dark wig. She hadn't been seen in her own colored hair for a while now, except in the privacy of her own home but that was okay. She felt the need to hide at least a small part of herself from the rest of the world, for her own protection.

She'd been in places like this most of her young life. Chicago wasn't any different than Raleigh in a way. There were seedy bars and run down neighborhoods all over the world, or at least her part of the world. She'd been born in Chicago twenty four years ago to a single mother. Her mother Carla had done the best she could being a single woman with no skills. Carla always tried to give her what she could but it didn't always work out the way either of them wanted.

Her father wasn't in the picture and never had been. Her mother always told her he left after only a week with her because he had a whole world yet to discover but as long as she had her mom, then everything seemed good. Carla told her once she tried to find him to tell him about the baby but she never could locate him.

It was only after her mother died when she was ten that her life went to hell. She'd known what being loved and cherished felt like when her mother had been alive and in one fleeting moment, she'd lost that feeling. As hard as she tried, she never found it again. The foster system was severely broken and she became one of the many who slipped through the cracks. She'd gone through six years of pure hell and the day she turned sixteen, she walked away from all the bullshit her life had been and made her own way in the world. Keeping herself hidden for the first two years had been hard but it was better than going back into the system.

Melora took a deep breath and blew it out. She didn't waste time thinking about the past. It was over and done...she couldn't change it. All she could do was pray and work for her future. As much as she wanted to deny it, she knew deep down in her heart, she had turned those feelings of hope into something else. She'd become tired of hurting so she wouldn't allow herself to feel at all. It was better that way. If she had no expectations, she never felt let down.

The air around her had cooled after the sun set and now it chilled her overheated skin. The sweat beading on her skin just five minutes ago, already dried on her face and she could feel her body cooling down. Flicking the cigarette away from her, she closed her eyes and rested for a moment before she went back to work.

When she heard the back door open, she groaned and ducked down behind the dumpster. She wasn't quite ready to go back inside yet. She frowned when she heard sounds of a struggle and peeked over the top of the dumpster that partially hid her.

Her eyes widened when she saw the five men move away from the doorway. Four of them belonged to the local MC, The Ghosts of Dixie while the fifth was Baily Walker. The four Ghosts of Dixie men were Whiskey, Micah, Jonesy and a man they called Lightning. They were four men she wouldn't want to run into alone that's for sure.

Of the four Ghosts of Dixie men, her eyes widened as she saw the man they called Whiskey throw a punch hitting Baily in the stomach. When Baily doubled over Whiskey drew the big ass knife he always carried from the sheath under the back of his jacket. Whiskey was known around town for this knife, it was something he always carried, and unfortunately, he was known to use it. The knife looked huge and as he twirled it in his hand, Melora saw the light gleam off the wide steel blade. The handle was hand carved ebony bone with their club emblem carved on it.

Melora watched as the four men circled Baily and Whiskey moved in. They were yelling at Baily telling him his uncle couldn't help him now. Baily tried to fight back but one man against four didn't stand a chance. He did connect one punch against Jonesy.

Jonesy faltered a step but came right back. His fist hit Baily in the jaw and before he could drop to the ground, Whiskey grabbed his shirt and held him up.

For a brief second, Melora thought the fight was over then she saw a certain look come over Whiskey. Crazy entered his eyes and Melora knew it wasn't going to end well for Baily. A look of pure rage passed across his features, the kind of rage only death could calm. It seemed as if someone else took him over as Whiskey's hand shot forward and the knife embedded itself in Baily's chest. Shock then severe pain could be seen on Baily's face as he crumbled to his knees. Whiskey shoved Baily away from him.

Melora gasped softly as she saw Baily hit the street. Blood pooled under him as his shirt suddenly turned from blue to purple as blood poured from the wound on his chest.

Ducking down behind the dumpster, she prayed none of the men had seen or heard her. Her heartbeat pounded in her chest and echoed loudly in her ears.

"What the fuck did you do, man?' Micah called out. Running his fingers through his hair as he stared at the body lying in front of him. "You weren't supposed to kill him! Raven isn't gonna like this. He warned us to beat some sense into him but not kill him. This little piece of shit owed him big money."

"Shut up you moron." Whiskey seethed. "Raven isn't gonna know shit. As long as nobody here tells him, he won't know the little shit is dead. We'll take the body out of town and dump him in the woods. He won't be found for months, if he's found at all. Wild hogs have been known to visit those woods."

"What are we gonna tell the boss?" Jonesy asked.

"We tell him we found him and passed along his message. He was alive and well the last we saw him," Whiskey told them. He looked over at Micah. "Go get the truck. We'll load him up and get the fuck out of here before anyone is the wiser."

Melora slid down until she was crouching behind the dumpster. She didn't want anyone to know she was there. Waiting until Micah backed the truck up to where Baily could be loaded into the truck bed, she watched as they got back in and took off.

She didn't wait any longer. She opened the back door of the bar then headed into the break room, she took her bag and jacket and left. She wasn't taking the chance of being discovered. She knew Whiskey wouldn't hesitate to silence her if he was aware of what she'd just witnessed.

Melora then ducked into the bar and grabbed her tip bucket.

Gloria glared at her as she poured another beer from the tap but Melora didn't care. She grabbed the bills in the bucket, stuffing them in her pocket she put the bucket back and left out the back door.

Running to her car, she got in and started the engine. Driving away, she sped through the near empty streets of Raleigh and made good time to her apartment.

The two bedroom apartment wasn't in a very good part of town but that never bothered her before tonight. Hurriedly, she unlocked the door and rushed inside. Entering her room, she got her duffle bag and began throwing her clothes inside. Opening her closet, she grabbed a couple of wigs she had there and stuffed them in as well. Then she went to her bathroom, lifted the cover for the toilet tank and reached inside, grabbing the baggie she'd hidden there.

Then she went to the kitchen and opened her freezer. Moving a few items, she grabbed the black pouch under the ice cream and slammed the door shut. Then she went to the coffee table in the middle of her living room. Reaching underneath she pulled out the drawer and carefully peeled off the envelope she taped there. One thing life had taught her was to always be prepared. She'd learned this lesson well enough to survive. She didn't dare even leave her roommate a note, the less she knew the better.

Pulling the duffle bag over her shoulder, she paused by the closet long enough to grab the smaller bag she'd packed already. Then without looking back, she left the place she called home for the last eighteen months.

She hoped her friend Izzy would understand her leaving but right now, she had no choice. Then it occurred to her she needed to make one more stop before she got the hell outta dodge.

~****~

Two years later found her in the town of Troy, New York. She'd become so tired of the mess her life had become. When she left Raleigh, she thought she was getting away safely but that hadn't been the case.

When Whiskey and the others came back to the bar Gloria asked them what happened in the alley. Everything went to hell after that.

When Melora called her a few days later, Gloria admitted the conversation with Whiskey. Gloria told her Whiskey was seriously pissed when he left. Gloria said she'd quit her job and was laying low until it blew over, whatever it was.

So, for the past two years Melora had been dodging Whiskey and his friends. Living in fear day after day, city after city. They'd almost found her in Charlotte and again, in Newport News. She'd barely gotten away from them in Dover and in Trenton. The last time they found her was six days ago in Boston.

She'd been working at a diner and was coming back from a bank run one afternoon. She'd parked her car in the back of the diner and walked through the back door when she heard Whiskey at the front counter asking about her. Keeping out of the hallway, she left the bank receipts on Herman's desk and slipped out the back door. She drove away like the devil had been after her. In truth, he was. An hour later, she called her old boss from a pay phone at a truck stop along the highway and quit her job.

Now she was in Troy, New York. She'd been here ever since, moving from place to place trying to keep out of trouble and still stay hidden.

Under the cover of darkness, she'd driven all over the city, searching for a place she could call home. She found an abandoned warehouse in the old part of town. Next door was a garage called Sin's Bastards Custom Motorcycles and she watched all day as members of the local MC came and went.

Keeping out of sight during the day wasn't a problem for her as she often left before the sun came up and stayed away until way after dark. She'd found several safe places to hang out during the daylight hours. One of them was a place called Redemption House. People came and went from there all day long. It was nothing for her to slip inside and watch the day to day comings and goings from there. At least there, she was out of the weather and could get something hot to eat. She'd been real careful not to be remembered and tried not to bring any attention to herself.

Then two days ago, something changed. She thought she heard the whine of Whiskey's cycle. She didn't know why but she could pick out the whine of his cycle over all the others she heard on a daily basis. It was almost as if it had its own sound that screamed, *evil is here...Look out.*

She looked around but couldn't find it. Just to be safe she stayed in the warehouse, out of sight until she could determine if Whiskey had indeed found her yet again. She hadn't heard his bike in a couple of days but that didn't mean he wasn't here.

Chapter One

Sam Tory rubbed the back of his neck and searched the area outside the shop. He kept getting the feeling of being watched for the last couple of days and it made him nervous. His eyes searched every nook and cranny but he didn't see anything out of place.

He felt a shiver run down his spine and he didn't enjoy it at all.

Sabbath stepped up to him. "What's up, Bones?"

"I'm not sure," Sam admitted. "Something's off."

"What are you talking about?"

Sam shrugged. "It's maybe nothing."

Sabbath stared at him for a minute then spoke, "You've always gone with your gut before, if something is telling you to watch your back, you need to watch your back." Pausing, he asked, "Are we in danger?"

Sam shook his head. "No I don't think so, I just have a feeling someone is watching us. I don't feel on edge, not yet anyway."

"I'll let the others know...Maybe with more than one pair of eyes we can find out what's going on."

"Yeah all right, but I don't want anyone panicking. We aren't under siege here. Like I said, I don't feel the danger but someone is watching. It's weird."

"I'll let the others know. We've trusted your intuition all these years, no reason not to now." Sabbath nodded and went back inside the shop.

Sam continued to stare at the area around the shop. He couldn't see anything but he knew someone was out there, watching him from the shadows.

~****~

Melora ducked back behind a column when his eyes came around to her building. She didn't know why but she'd felt this man's eyes on hers a couple of times.

He was a big guy, at least six foot four inches tall. His body was well built and he looked like he could move a mountain. His dark hair was a little on the long side as it hung down his back and was brushed away from his face caught up in a short ponytail.

He wore jeans and a t-shirt under an MC cut. He'd been too far away to see which MC he belonged to but it didn't surprise Melora much. A lot of people she knew or had seen in the last few years were involved with motorcycle clubs. She didn't know why but she had a feeling this guy just fit with an MC. He just seemed the type. Just her luck.

She moved deeper into the building while rubbing her arms. The damp musty air in the warehouse made her cold.

Going back to the area she'd been living in, she laid down on her sleeping bag. It'd been three days since she heard the whine of Whiskey's pipes but she hadn't seen him yet. Staying out of sight was getting harder and harder. She was tired of living with this fear day after day and the last two years were getting old. She was past the point of wanting her life back.

She heard her stomach growl. Groaning, she got to her feet and moved over to where her food stash was. Looking through what she had, she didn't find anything she really wanted to eat. She gave up and went back to the window. Glancing over at the shop again, she noted no one was there.

Going to another window she searched for the older guy she'd seen watching her. She didn't spot him, but she knew he was probably still there.

Gazing up at the sky, she noted it looked dark gray. It was late in the year and she knew she would have to find a warmer place if she was going to stay here for the winter. Snow would soon be a problem.

Already, the nights were colder than she could stand. She really hated being cold. Hungry she could handle but cold? It seemed to settle deep in her bones and it was hard to get warmed up again.

She thought about moving over to Redemption House but she couldn't afford anyone doing the paperwork. In order to remain anonymous she couldn't leave any kind of paper trail behind. She shivered as a gust of cold air came in through a broken window just down from where she stood.

Melora went over to her stuff and hauled a coat out of the pile. Bringing it around her shoulders, she immediately felt warmer. Bringing her hands up to her mouth, she blew warm air on them. She hadn't realized how chilled she was until now.

Wandering back over to the windows, she glanced back to the shop and watched as everyone left the parking lot. The last one out locked the doors and as the sun went down, everything around her fell quiet.

Melora decided to check the shop out. She hoped there would be facilities she could borrow for a shower and a hot meal. Grabbing her small bag, she left her warehouse and made her way across the distance. She went around to a back window and tried to slide the glass upward. Surprised the window actually moved, she quickly moved inside and slid the window closed.

Knowing she couldn't turn the lights on she grabbed a small flashlight from her bag and flipped it on. Moving around the inside, she found herself in some kind of office. Not interested in the inner workings of a garage she quickly moved further into the belly of the shop.

The next room she came to looked like some sort of kitchenette and break room. She found a fridge, stove and microwave. Glancing into the fridge, she found some containers with food inside. Checking out the freezer section, she found several frozen pizzas and when she found them, her stomach growled. She hadn't had a hot meal for a few days and a bubbling hot pizza in an even longer time.

Hoping no one minded, she grabbed one and turned the oven on. While the pizza baked, she continued with her search. She did find a full bath next door to the kitchen and she shivered as she dreamed of having a hot shower.

She didn't care about anything else. She wasn't here to steal or make any trouble. When the timer on the stove went off, she went back to the kitchen. Fifteen minutes later, Melora ate the last piece of the pizza and threw her garbage in the trash. The hot food filled her belly but also filled something else, something she hadn't realized was low. It had given her almost a feeling of normalcy.

Checking the clock, she saw it was getting late. She grabbed her bag, then went back to the bathroom and quickly stripped her clothes off. Taking off the wig, she unbraided her natural hair and combed it out with her fingers. Her natural hair color was so pale it was almost silver and it flowed down her back almost to the floor. She had to hide it as the color and the length would have made her stick out of the norm. Not very many people knew what exactly she hid under all the wigs she wore and this suited Melora just fine.

Keeping her hair this long was a promise she'd made to her mother a very long time ago. She remembered being a child and her mother was brushing her hair. Carla had always told her long hair was a woman's glory. Her own hair was almost down to her hips and whenever she brushed her daughter's hair she often told her, she had her daddy's coloring. Her pale blonde almost white hair and violet eyes belonged to the man who donated the sperm that created her.

Melora felt more than a little mad at the man who helped create her and then left town but Carla told her that's just the way he was. He hadn't been ready to be a father yet and she wouldn't trade her for all the world. Melora knew her mother loved her and while she only had her for a little while, she never forgot her.

So, Melora never cut her hair as a tribute to the woman who gave her life. She hid her glory from the rest of the world but that was her secret.

When she stepped under the warm spray, she moaned. The heat from the water partially thawed the solid ice her body had become. As she soaped her body and hair, Melora rushed through the pleasure of her shower. As much as she wished she didn't have to hurry, she knew the men arrived early for work and she couldn't take the chance at being caught.

Fifteen minutes later, Melora was braiding her hair again and hiding it under her dark colored wig. Cleaning up behind herself, she finally shut the lights off behind her and made her way to the back window. She didn't want anyone to know she'd been there as it would defeat the purpose of her hiding out.

Peeking out into the night, she saw there was no one around. Sliding the glass pane up, she slipped out and closed the window behind her. She felt better than she had an hour ago but she also knew Whiskey might be out there waiting for her.

She didn't know how he kept finding her as her trail had been one of necessity rather than planned but every time she stopped along the way, he'd been almost right behind her. She'd changed her vehicle three times now, worked just enough to keep her from starving and lived out of her vehicle instead of finding an apartment.

She was almost to the point of giving up then she thought about what Whiskey would do to her if she did. Him and that damn wicked knife of his. There must be more to life than just living in fear.

Focused on making it back to the warehouse, she quietly made her way forward, then happened to glance back. Damn, her footprints were showing. There had been a light dusting of snow the day before. She couldn't afford anyone finding her, so grabbing a tree limb she backtracked her own tracks and began sweeping the evidence away.

She barely made it back to the warehouse she'd been staying at when she heard the first bike coming closer. Dawn had barely broke but she could see the morning light brightening everything around her. Ducking in the building, she watched carefully as the biker stopped next door. As she watched him get off his bike and take off his helmet, she found herself staring at the older guy she saw the day before. For some damned reason, she couldn't take her eyes off him.

He stood as tall and big as she remembered. Today, he wore jeans and a green t-shirt under his jacket and cut. His dark hair was brushed away from his face and it looked fine as it was pulled back into a short ponytail again. She couldn't help but wonder what his hair would look like hanging free. Would it curl around his neck and shoulders? Melora sighed deep as she stared at him. She wasn't normally interested in older men but there was just something about this one that made her insides go gooey. She wished she were in a position to at least meet the man. She turned away and went back to where her things were. There was no sense in thinking like this. Meeting him would be a real bad idea. Bikers were what got her into this trouble in the first damn place. Putting the small bag on the floor, she laid down and tried to sleep.

~****~

Sam searched the area around the shop. He felt the eyes watching him again and the feeling was beginning to creep him out. He walked around the perimeter of the building looking for any sign of an intruder. He couldn't help it, something seemed off and he needed to find out what.

He didn't find anything until he got back by the windows to the office. That's when he noticed the whole area in the back of the shop had been brushed. Not only was a path brushed free of footprints, the whole area had been cleared. He couldn't tell in which direction this someone had come or gone from, but they had come through here. The marks in the fresh snow weren't there by accident but by design.

Someone was covering his tracks and now Sam knew someone had definitely been watching them. The only thing he didn't know was why and who. This just pissed him the hell off.

Growling, he went back to the front door. Unlocking it, he swung the main door open and snapped on the lights.

Looking carefully for some sigh of an intruder, he didn't see anything out of place. Then he got to the kitchen. At first, he didn't see anything. The countertops were wiped down and the stove felt cool to the touch. Then he smelled it. The scent was very faint, almost gone in fact but he caught the scent of melted cheese and tomatoes.

Going to the garbage can, he found the empty pizza box. Knowing no one in the shop had baked a pizza in the last few days, the box in the trash didn't make sense.

He quickly went to the office and checked the moneybox. Nothing seemed to be disturbed but this didn't give him any comfort. In fact, it disturbed him a bit. If someone had broken in, surely they would have searched for the moneybox, wouldn't they?

He heard the others in the main part of the shop and replaced the moneybox then joined them.

Iceman, Sabbath and Raine were there.

Sam didn't want anyone else to know what he'd found, so he didn't mention it. He needed time to get to the bottom of it first, before he said anything.

He saw Sabbath stare at him briefly but he shook his head. Sabbath might be wise to what he thought was going on but he didn't want to put his feelings into words. He would just keep an eye out for potential problems.

Several times that day, the hairs on the back of Sam's neck stood out but he couldn't find anything out of the ordinary. He'd searched the entire building several times and found nothing more. He even went to the top two floors but found nothing up there either. Not even a footprint in the dust.

Late that afternoon, Sabbath found him. "So what's going on with you today, Bones?"

Sam shrugged. "I'm not sure."

"Did you find something the rest of us should be aware of?"

Again, Sam shrugged. He got up and went to the main door again. Looking out over the dooryard, he couldn't find anything out of place yet again. He turned and stared at Sabbath. "When I got here this morning I took a walk around the building. The entire back had been purposely brushed clean."

"What do you mean brushed clean?"

"I mean someone had taken the time to brush the entire back area clean of footprints of any kind, human or otherwise." Sam shook his head. "Then I checked the shop and office. The money box hadn't been touched and there was nothing in the shop either but when I went into the kitchen this morning, I found a pizza box in the trash."

"And that bothered you?" Sabbath looked surprised.

Exhaling a deep breath, Sam replied, "No not really, anyone could have baked it but I thought I could smell it in the air yet. Why would I be able to smell pizza at six in the morning and the place had been locked up all night?"

"Damned if I know." Sabbath looked around.

"Don't say anything to the others just yet. I don't want them to know until I can find out what's going on. It may be nothing."

"What are you going to do?"

Sam shrugged. "I'm not sure yet."

Sabbath nodded. "Well, let me know if you need help to figure this out.

"Yeah." Sam let out a frustrated sigh. "I'm not sure what I need at this point."

Sabbath walked away and one by one, the guys left for the day.

Sam brought his bike inside and locked the main door as usual. Shutting off the lights, he settled in for the night.

Three different times during the night, he made his rounds. Walking around the shop and office with only a small flashlight he found nothing. When he settled down in the break room to catch a nap, he closed his eyes and fell into a light sleep.

It could have been five minutes or three hours later when something woke him. Sam's eyes remained closed but his hearing picked up the slight sound from outside the room. It sounded like a soft sliding of a window being raised. Soundlessly, he got to his feet and went to the door. Slipping off his boots, he padded quietly down the hall pausing outside the office.

He could hear someone moving around inside as he pressed himself against the wall waiting for whoever was in the office to walk through the doorway. The footsteps came closer and Sam held his breath until he saw a shadow moving toward him. With no light in the building, the shadow passed very close to where he stood. As it passed him, Sam reached out and wrapped his arms around the slight figure in front of him.

Dropping down to the floor he heard a scream but it didn't register this was a female until the small figure below him began to fight back. "Hold it lady, I don't want to hurt you!" Sam spoke in her ear.

"Then get the bloody hell off me!" the woman shouted as she tried and failed to buck him off.

"Not yet sweetheart." Sam held her down. "Tell me what you think you're doing in here first."

"Get fucked." She squirmed in his hold. "I didn't steal anything and I don't have to tell you shit."

"Wrong answer sweetheart." Sam pressed her down on the floor.

"Let me go!" She fought back.

Sam was stronger than she was though. "Not a chance." He got to his feet and pulled her up. Grasping her by the upper arms, he pushed her into the break room. He flipped on the light, then shoved her down into a chair. Breathing heavily, he looked her over carefully.

She was dressed in jeans and a winter jacket. She had some kind of small backpack looped around one shoulder. She was petite and her glittery eyes were wide in her face.

Cute was a word he might use to describe her, but she also looked enraged. He studied her and felt his body harden. Oh, to hell with that. This chick could be here to do him or his men in. In his hard life, it wouldn't be the first time someone sent a woman to do the job either.

~* * * *~

Melora glared at him. She recognized him as the older biker she'd been watching the last couple of days. Up close, he was even better looking than she noticed before, his hair brushed back from his face had come out of the ponytail he usually wore and flowed down to his shoulders. Its dark color was sprinkled with grey but it didn't make him look old, it just gave him character.

His eyes were light blue and at the moment, drawn together in suspicion. His build looked bigger this close than she remembered. At least six foot four to her five foot two, he towered over her...and well built too. His muscles corded down his arms and she could see his chest was well defined. She could see part of a skull tattoo that went up his bicep. The t-shirt he wore barely covered his upper body. The material was stretched tight over his muscles. She licked her lips at the sight.

He moved away from the door and pulled out another chair to sit beside her.

Melora took the second he went to grab the chair to bolt toward the door.

Before she could get three steps away, he grabbed her around the waist and hauled her back to her chair. "You aren't going anywhere little girl, until I get some answers."

Melora glared at him. "I'm not your little girl and I already told you I don't have to answer to you or anyone." She crossed her legs and continued to glare at him. "Do your worst."

He narrowed his eyes and crossed his arms over his chest. "Honey, be careful of what you ask for, you might just get it."

"I'm not afraid of you." She sneered. "In fact, I could use a night in jail. At least it's warm there."

He frowned. "Where have you been staying that's so cold?"

"None of your freakin business."

"Why did you break in here?"

Melora turned her head away, so she wouldn't have to answer his question.

"Have you been in here before tonight?" He yanked the bag from her shoulder and flopped it down on the table behind her. Moving closer to it, he unzipped the bag and taking his eyes off her, he peeked inside.

The bag held a towel and soap along with a microwave meal. He frowned and pulled everything out of the bag.

Melora glanced at him and found his attention on the items she'd brought with her. Eyeing the door, she calculated her chances and decided now was a good time. She bolted for the door again, this time, making it out through the door and down the hall before he caught her.

When his arm circled her waist, she screamed in frustration and grabbed the closest doorway to try to avoid being hauled back into the break room. It didn't work but she tried.

When he got her back to her chair, he shoved her down into it. "Don't you fuckin move! If you try and run again, I'll tie your pretty little ass up," he warned as he paced in front of her.

Melora glared at him. "Why don't you just call the cops and get this over with?"

He rolled his eyes at her. "I don't call the cops sugar. If I called anyone it would be my brothers and I don't want to do that yet." He pulled a chair out and sat down in front of her. "I want to know why you've been watching this place for the last few days."

"Who says I have?"

"I do," he assured her with a cold tone. "I've felt you watching us and I want to know why."

Melora shrugged.

"Where have you been staying?"

She just stared at him.

"What is your name?"

Her stare never faltered nor did she blink.

His frustration was obvious. Running his fingers through his hair, he coldly whispered, "If I call the brothers in you *will* answer my questions. They aren't as nice about this sort of thing as I have been."

Melora snorted. "You don't scare me Mr. Biker Man. I've been dealing with your sort of trash my whole life."

He pulled his boots back on, then getting to his feet he unbuckled his belt.

Melora knew a moment of fear but it didn't show on her face.

Grasping her arm, he pulled her to her feet. Swinging her around, he grabbed her wrists and wrapped the belt around them. With her hands secured behind her, he gripped her arm and backpack then hauled her to the front door. Shutting off the lights behind them, he led her out to a truck sitting in the yard. Pushing her inside, he locked the door behind her then got in the truck and started the engine. Pulling out to the main road, he drove in silence.

Melora tried to wiggle her hands free but all it did was tighten the belt until she couldn't feel her hands anymore. When the truck stopped, she stared at the small house sitting off the dirt road. They'd driven out of the city but not too far. She could still see the city lights in the distance behind her. The house wasn't very big but it looked nice. A cute small one story house, painted blue with grey trim. She could see a wraparound porch and a garage. Smoke rose from the chimney.

'Mr. Silent Biker Trash' came around the truck and helped her out. Leading her all the way to the front door, he dug in his pocket for his keys. Opening the door, he pushed her inside and turned on the lights.

The open floor plan disclosed an area for the living room, dining room and small kitchen. Off to the left were three doors. The open door showed it was a bedroom with a huge king size bed in it. The second door was a bathroom and the third door was closed.

Still silent, he took off his jacket and grabbed her hands, unraveling the belt.

Melora moved away from him but didn't go far. She turned to watch him. "What is this place? Who lives here?"

"I do," he admitted. Moving over to the kitchen, he took down two glasses and reached for a bottle of whiskey on the counter. Pouring a generous amount in the glasses, he pushed one toward her and lifted the other to his lips.

Melora grabbed the glass and downed the liquor. It burned down her throat and warmed her belly. Slamming the glass down, she asked, "So now what?"

"Are you hungry?"

Pausing, she narrowed her eyes and stared at him for a moment then shrugged. "I could eat."

Looking amused, he went to the fridge. Taking out a dozen eggs, he went to the stove and a few minutes later, he took out two plates and scooped the scrambled eggs out of the pan and onto the plates. He picked up a couple forks, then ushered her to a table and set the plates down. Sitting on a chair, he began to eat.

Melora sat down and grabbed her fork. A moment later, she was shoving the food into her mouth. It might only be scrambled eggs but it was hot and filling.

While she ate, he set a glass of juice down beside her.

When her plate was clean, she took it over to the sink and rinsed it off. Sitting down again, she waited for him to make his next move.

When he stood up, he motioned for her to go toward the bedroom.

Dragging her feet, she stepped closer.

He pulled her away at the last minute. "Not my room, you'll sleep here." He opened the only closed door.

Suspicious, Melora peeked inside. It was another bedroom. When she walked in, she could see a bed and dresser as well as a closet. There was one small window. She turned to face him.

He just studied her for a moment then shaking his head, he moved back closing the door behind him.

She waited for a moment and sure enough...she heard a lock snap shut. He'd locked her in. Shrugging, she moved over to the window and tried to lift the pane. It wouldn't lift and looked like it had been nailed shut. She groaned as she realized she was trapped here at least for what remained of the night.

Taking off her jacket, she went over to the bed and laid down. Moaning with pleasure, she couldn't help but relish the softness beneath her. It'd been far too long since she slept in a bed. It felt like heaven to her. Sitting up, she shimmed out of her jeans and bra, then crawled under the covers with a huge sigh and closed her eyes.

Chapter Two

The sun was shining in through the window when Melora woke a few hours later. Peeking out of the covers, she looked over at the door...unlocked and opened. Pushing the blankets back, she retrieved her jeans, bra and boots and put them on. Then she went over to the door and gazed out into the main room.

She saw Mr. Biker sitting at the table with the newspaper and a cup of coffee. Squaring her shoulders, she stepped out and joined him.

When she sat down beside him, he got up and without a word, he poured her a cup of coffee.

Melora sipped the hot brew and almost groaned as the coffee slid down her throat.

He chuckled but didn't say anything as he sat back down and continued to read his paper.

"Don't you have to go to work or something?" she finally asked.

"I'm not going in today."

"Why?"

He lowered his paper and glared at her. "Because you haven't told me anything yet, sweetheart. I want to know why you broke into the shop and who you are. Until you start talking, you and I aren't going anywhere."

"What difference does it make who I am?" Melora shouted, getting to her feet. "I didn't take anything or destroy anything in your precious shop. I took a hot shower and baked a pizza...that's all I did. Why can't you just leave it and me alone?"

Sam shook his head. "Why were you watching us the past two days?"

"I don't know...no reason really." She shrugged as she sat back down in her chair.

"You can do better than that honey." Sam scoffed.

"I had nothing better to do," she offered as she drained her coffee cup dry.

He snorted with disbelief.

Melora grinned. "Maybe I was admiring your very buff physique."

He narrowed his eyes and stared at her. "Watch what you say darling, I doubt you can handle what I got."

Melora snorted. "I very much doubt that, old man," she whispered.

Abrupt like, he got up and came over to her. He stopped beside her then grasped the back of her neck. Quietly, he pulled her to her feet and closer to him. He watched her eyes for a moment then leaned toward her and pressed his mouth over hers.

At first, it was just their lips crushed together but when a zing went through her body, she gasped, opening her mouth to him. Thrusting his tongue deep into her mouth the kiss turned hot. He crushed her body to his and Melora felt on fire. His mouth, his tongue, his hands burned her skin as the kiss deepened.

Melora felt something let go inside her as her core went from warm to lava hot in an instant. Her body wanted more. Her hands went to his neck and she pulled him even closer. He groaned as his lips dragged down to her neck. His teeth began nipping and sucking on her skin.

Melora gasped and dragged his face back up as she initiated another kiss. Then she tore herself away from his embrace. Breathing heavily, she stared at him for a moment then turned and ran back to her room, slamming the door behind her.

Melora flopped down on the bed and let the tears flow. She was still stunned at her body's betrayal. Never before did a kiss turn her on like that one had. She was twenty four years old but had never felt the overwhelming need to share her body with another. Her mother had talked to her about love and while she'd never felt it for anyone before, she often thought about it.

She remembered her mother telling her it was easy to use her body as an escape from loneliness and Melora had promised her she would never do that. It'd been a promise she found easy to keep before, but now—maybe not.

This biker man might be older than she was but she wanted him. He didn't love her and she didn't love him but he awoke something inside her that wouldn't and couldn't be ignored.

A while later, he knocked on her door.

She heard him call out 'breakfast is ready' and Melora wasn't sure she even felt hungry, but her body needed substance. She knew she needed to eat to keep her strength up. When she opened the door, she saw him already sitting at the table eating.

Quietly, she sat down and stared at her plate. He'd scrambled eggs, cooked bacon and made toast. The aroma of the food gave her an appetite and she dug in. When the food went into her mouth, she moaned. She cleared her plate within minutes,

Shaking his head, he chuckled.

Melora blushed. "Well, what did you expect? It's been awhile since I had a hot meal."

"Are you ready to tell me who you are yet?"

She shrugged. "I'm nobody."

"Why do I doubt that very much?"

Melora sat back and glared at him. "What difference will a name make? I'm out of here as soon as you let me go anyway."

"Who says I'm letting you go?" he asked softly.

"Why would you keep me?" she frowned. "I'm not important."

"You intrigue me."

Melora snorted. She wanted to say something but it wasn't very nice and she was at his mercy.

His lips thinned when he caught her look. "Be very careful what you say next baby girl, you might not like how I retaliate."

She watched him for a moment then she decided to stay on the defensive with this man. Her lips curled up into a smile. "You must be getting old, old man. It doesn't take much to interest you."

His eyes narrowed almost to slits at her taunts. Apparently, she had no idea who she was talking to. He got to his feet, stretching up to his impressive six foot four inches tall. Reaching out, he yanked her up by the upper arm and hauled her over to his sofa. Sitting down, he pulled her across his lap. When she yelped, his hand came down on her backside and the slap echoed in the small house.

Melora was furious. "How dare you? Let me up this instant, you bastard!" She screamed as she fought to get free.

Instead of releasing her, he reached down underneath her and unbuttoned her jeans then grabbing the waistband from the back, he pulled them down to bare her ass.

Melora screamed again as his palm came down on her bare ass. Again and again, his hand came down on her skin.

After a dozen or so swats, her body was on fire but for a different reason. Her ass was probably red and aflame but she felt something else altogether, something very primitive. While the spanking was meant as punishment, her body reacted to it in another way. And apparently so did his. She could feel him against her side. He was rock hard.

~****~

When she stormed out after the kiss, earlier today Sam had stood there in the kitchen staring at the closed door. His breathing was heavy and his body felt hard. His cock throbbed in his pants. He hadn't felt like this in a very long time. He had to adjust himself as he sat down on the chair and ran his fingers through his hair. He needed to let his body settle down. He couldn't get involved with this girl. Yeah, she was young but all woman as he just found out. But females were trouble and he didn't need that kind of grief in his life. He promised himself he wouldn't get caught up with her.

Now, here he sat after smacking her well rounded ass but good Sam realized his hand began caressing her red ass, smoothing over her spanked skin. His fingers dipped to her core and he could feel her wetness. He groaned as he sank his fingers inside her. Remembering the earlier kiss, his body caught fire and he wanted her like he'd never wanted another woman before.

Moving his fingers in and out of her, he watched as her body responded.

She opened her legs, almost welcoming his intrusion. She moaned and wiggled her hips in time to his rhythm. Then suddenly, she pushed back against his hand and her body tightened against his fingers.

Sam nearly growled as she came on his fingers and he felt her sweet body tighten against his hand. He pushed her off his lap and got to his feet. Striding to his bedroom, he closed the door before he did something he would regret.

~*****~

Melora sat on the floor stunned. She couldn't believe what just happened. She'd never felt an orgasm as strong as the one she'd just had. Her eyes rose to his closed door and she had to wonder what he would do if she joined him there.

Her legs felt weak as she stood up and got dressed again. Her ass was tender but not overly sore and she thought maybe she did deserve what he'd done. She had treated him like an ass. The spanking anyway, the orgasm was something else altogether.

She went over to the door and opened it. She didn't enter the room but instead stood in the doorway. He had his back to her and before he could turn around she whispered, "They call me Melora."

~*****~

Sam heard the door close behind her and he closed his eyes. Melora, yeah it fit her...if it was her real name in any case. This girl was hiding something and he intended to find out what.

His body was still primed but he knew he couldn't control it, at least not yet. He didn't go after her, he just prayed she would still be there when he did come out of his room.

A couple of hours later, he opened his door and went out to the living room. The scent of tomato sauce and garlic bread met him and his stomach growled in hunger. He paused and watched as Melora stirred a pot of noodles on the stove.

She made no sign of knowing he was there but she reached for a plate and dished him up some spaghetti. Topping off the noodles with the sauce, she paired it with homemade garlic bread and set it down on the table. A moment later, she sat down with another plate and wordlessly began to eat.

Sam joined her and the first mouthful made him groan in pleasure. The sauce was like nothing he'd ever had before. Spices burst in his mouth and he couldn't shovel it in fast enough. Even the bread was good, hot, buttery and garlicky, yet crunchy. Pushing his chair back, he sighed as he rubbed his stomach. "I can't believe you found all of this in my cupboards."

Melora shrugged. "I like to cook, what can I say?"

"I like to eat, what can I say?" Sam grinned.

Melora stared at him for a moment. "I really can't stay here long."

"Why? What are you running from?"

Melora squirmed in her seat. "It's not so much a what as a who," she finally admitted.

Sam grimaced. "Okay, *who* are you running from?"

Melora got up without answering and began putting leftovers away. When the dishes were washed and dried, she turned to face him. "Well, I'm going to bed now. It's late and I'm tired."

Sam raised an eyebrow. "It's barely seven."

~****~

Melora shrugged at him. She didn't answer and went to her bedroom. Her nerves were shot. Thinking a shower might help her unwind. She went to the dresser and began opening the drawers for something to wear to bed. She found an old t-shirt. Kicking off her boots, she went to the door and peeked out into the living room. She didn't see him, so she walked across the hall into the bathroom and shut the door behind her.

Moments later, the hot water poured over her. Melora sighed with relief as the warmth spread to encase her. She'd never known cold the way she'd known it the last two years. Living on the run with Whiskey behind her all the way, left her living in fear. She hated it. A person shouldn't have to live with fear every day.

Scrubbing her skin with warm water felt so good. Washing her hair felt even better. She frowned as she stared at the brown wig she'd been wearing for far too long. Her eyes went to the mirror above the sink and she couldn't help but stare at her reflection.

Her long unbound white blonde hair flowed down her back past her butt and ended almost on the floor of the shower. She'd had to hide her unique coloring. Too many people would remember someone with her coloring and she couldn't afford to be remembered. She did her best to blend in and not be remembered.

Her violet eyes were a feature she couldn't hide though. She could shove everything else under clothing and wigs so no one really knew what she looked like and that was her protection. The only way she could feel safe.

Toweling off, she began to braid her long hair. Fitting the wig back on was a pain in the ass but she would do it to keep herself safe. She went back to her room and laid down on the bed. Moonlight came through the windows but she couldn't sleep. Her body was still sizzling with feelings left over from the punishment Biker Man had given her earlier. She was wearing just a t-shirt to bed because she'd washed her underwear after her shower.

Moaning softly she reached down and began to touch herself. That didn't satisfy or bring back the feelings of his hands on her skin. Frustrated, Melora stared at her door and wondered if she had the courage to go to him.

Without another thought, she threw back the covers and went to her door. Somewhere in the house, a clock chimed the time. Eleven bells. She didn't think she had moved but swiftly she was outside his bedroom door. Reaching for the knob, she turned it and went inside.

Stopping at the side of the bed, she reached up and pulled the shirt from her shoulders. Lifting the covers, she slid in beside him. His hot body warmed her and she leaned over his chest. When her lips found his in the dark, her body burst into flames.

~* * * *~

Sam heard his door open as he laid there, his fists ready for anything that came toward him. When the moonlight lit the shadows and he saw it was Melora, he felt only half surprised. He watched as she lifted her shirt and he stared at her naked body before she climbed into his bed. He wasn't sure this was a good idea but when her lips touched his in the dark, all thought fled his mind and his libido took over. His body hardened as her tongue swept inside his mouth. Suddenly, nothing else mattered but exploring the woman who'd come voluntarily to his bed.

His hand came up and cupped her breast. They were just the right size to fit into his hands. Her breasts were full and taut and he groaned as his thumbs flicked over her nipples. He could feel her moist heat as she rubbed her hot pussy on his thigh, dry humping his leg.

Flipping her on her back, he settled into the space between her legs. He backed off her mouth long enough to whisper, "Are you sure about this?"

Melora shushed him and kissed him again, thrusting her tongue in his mouth. After a long moment, she pulled her mouth away. "Please," she whispered against his lips, "Please fuck me."

Sam's hand went down to guide him where they both wanted him to be. When the tip of his cock entered her, he pushed in deep. So deep, he almost didn't notice the barrier he broke. He stopped.

Melora's legs curled around his waist and held him there. "Please don't stop now. I need you not to stop," she begged.

Sam could feel how tight she was and in a moment, he didn't really care. He pushed in the rest of the way and began the time old rhythm. With each stroke, he went in deeper. He fit inside her like a glove and he wasn't a small man. He ground his body against hers and she groaned but met his every thrust.

His hand went down and rubbed her clit, he was so very close but wanted her to go first. He wanted to feel her explode around him before he gave her his all. When he felt the walls of her pussy begin to pulse, he began to stroke her harder and faster. He was like a rushing train, eager to get to the end of the tunnel. He couldn't stop or slow down now if he wanted to.

Melora screamed out as her body exploded. She arched her back and ground herself into him.

Sam couldn't hold back any longer. He shot off inside her like never before. His mouth crashed down on hers and he held her close for a long moment.

When he rolled off to her side, he held her close while his heart calmed down. His hands rubbed up and down her back.

"Oh my god..." she whispered into his chest. "That was like—wow, I can't even d-describe it."

Sam chuckled. "Thanks...I think?"

Melora touched her lips to his chest. "Thank you. Now, I know what I've been missing all these years."

Sam tightened his arms around her. "I have to ask, why me?"

Melora sighed. For a moment, she didn't say anything at all then she told him, "In all my life, I've never met a man I wanted to share my body with. My mother always told me it was something special to share it with someone you loved. I know I don't love you and you don't love me, but this is the first time I've ever felt like this with any man and I wanted to know where this would go. Besides, I feel safe with you and that means something to me. Does that make any sense to you?"

Sam nodded. "Yeah, in its own curious way it does make sense. I don't know why but thank you."

Melora closed her eyes and relaxed her body...like she felt safe in his arms.

Sam closed his eyes and smiled. Whoever she was, she felt like she belonged right here. He even thought about keeping her. A rare thing for him to ever consider doing.

Chapter Three

The sun was barely up the next morning when Sam smoothed his hands over her satiny skin.

Without opening her eyes, Melora arched her back giving him access to the places she wanted him to touch. His fingers slipped inside her and she groaned as he went in deep. His lips nibbled on her neck as she pushed her ass against his hard hot cock.

"Fuck me," she whispered.

"Gladly." He growled with need as he placed himself between her legs. Opening her legs wider, he pushed himself deep inside her core. She was wet and eager for him and he obliged her. Each stroke gave her more of what he had and she moaned.

He felt her body tighten and he couldn't help but dig in deeper and harder with each plunge inside her. He knew he was probably leaving small bruises on her hips but he couldn't help himself. He'd never been a gentle lover. Her nipples hardened into pebbles and he moaned as they scraped his chest. He felt a tightening in his balls and knew it wouldn't take much to push him over the edge but he wanted her to come first. Slipping his hand down between them, he rubbed her clit and almost immediately, felt her body clamp down on his.

Sam rammed deep inside her and felt his cum flood her. He didn't know where she quit and he began and the orgasm lasted a long time. As their bodies cooled, he felt her shiver beneath him. Rolling to her side, he chuckled as she sighed.

"You know for an old man you know what you're doing," she murmured.

"I'm not really all *that* old," Sam grumbled. "And my name is Sam."

"Well, Sam..." She let out a slow easy breath. "...You sure know how to show a girl a good time. I almost hate to leave."

"You aren't going anywhere," he assured her.

Melora tried to get out of bed. "You can't keep me here."

Sam held her down. "Wanna bet?" he growled. "You still haven't answered my questions."

Melora looked up at him. "Please just let me go. I'll disappear and you'll never see me again. You really don't want me to stay."

Sam reached out and brushed the hair out of her face. "Who are you running from baby girl and why? Maybe I can help you."

Melora shook her head. "You don't want to get involved in my troubles. It's not worth it, I'm not worth it. It's too dangerous. I don't want you to get hurt."

"How about you let me decide what I want to get mixed up in?" Sam murmured. "I just don't want you to run away from me and I have a feeling if I let you go, that's just what you'll do."

Melora leaned forward and kissed his lips. Before she or Sam could deepen it, she bolted away from him. When she got to the door, she touched her fingers to her lips and whispered, "I think I'll take a shower."

Sam watched her go and when she was gone, he flopped back down on the bed. Running his hand over his forehead he listened to the water begin running. Throwing the blankets back, he got up and went to his dresser. Grabbing a clean pair of jeans and a t-shirt he went to the bathroom door and opened it. He could see her in the shower. Setting his clothes down, he opened the shower door and stepped inside.

~****~

Melora gasped when he joined her but she didn't object. His hands began touching her body and it felt so good. She was still wearing the wig, so she hadn't gotten her hair wet. The steam from the hot water was making her head itch but with him standing beside her, she couldn't scratch. When he traded places under the water, she moved away and let him wash up.

She was about to step out when he pulled her back. His lips nibbled on the back of her neck as his hands came around and cupped her breasts. "Why is it I want you again when I just had you?" he whispered in her ear.

"I don't know." She closed her eyes against his assault. "But who am I to deny you?"

Sam pushed her against the shower wall and his feet moved her legs apart. Then he plunged inside her from behind, deep and hard. He didn't stop and each thrust went deeper and harder.

Melora moaned as her body quickly went from warm to hot. When he pushed inside her, her core was wet and slippery. Each plunge of him went deep and she loved it. She'd seen men before in her life and so she knew he was bigger than most men and yet she handled his size easily.

She felt herself tighten as she drew closer and she couldn't help but push back against him. He ground into her and she felt her body explode. Closing her eyes against the feeling, she saw white dots melding into brilliant colors as she came hard.

Sam groaned as she clamped down on his cock, his hot cum flooding her. He hung his head and let the water rush over his head and shoulders.

Melora opened the door and slipped out but he didn't go after her. Instead, he turned his head and watched as she dried off.

Wrapping a towel around her, she left the bathroom and went back to her room. Dressing in the clothes she'd worn the day before made her grimace but she did it. Her panties from the night before were still a little damp. Slipping on her shoes, she tidied her room and stepped into the living area.

Sam was already there and making coffee when she joined him. Even fully dressed she could see he was in good shape. She couldn't help but compare him to the other men she knew.

Whiskey might think he was buff but Sam *really* was well built. His shoulders were wide and muscular, his chest wide and tight, his arms could crush her, yet they held her safe all night. His thighs were big and hard, his hands were huge and rough but they also knew how to bring her pleasure. Melora sighed.

Sam put a cup of coffee in front of her and asked, "What's the sigh for?"

She picked up the cup and without looking at him said, "I really need to go back to the shop."

"Why? What's at the shop?"

"I was staying at the warehouse in the back," she admitted. "I need to get my things and get back on the road."

"Again, I'll ask who exactly is after you and why?"

She just stared at him for a moment then asked, "You aren't going to just let this go are you?"

Sam grinned and shook his head.

"Why? What difference does my life make to you?" she whispered.

He shrugged but didn't say anything.

Melora squirmed in her chair. Then she got up, went to the window and looked outside. "Two years ago, I saw a man named Whiskey knife another man. He found out I saw him and he's been after me ever since. It seems no matter where I go, he finds me. I've been in this town for way too long. If I don't leave soon, he'll find me. Then he'll kill me to keep his crime a secret."

"Where did this go down?"

"Raleigh, North Carolina."

"Were you the only witness?"

Melora shook her head. "There were three other men standing there."

"And they let it happen?" Sam frowned.

Melora snorted. "They all wore the same cut."

Sam's frown deepened. "What club did they belong too?"

"The Ghosts of Dixie."

"Did the President order the hit?"

Melora shrugged. "I have no idea but something tells me he didn't."

"What was that?"

She turned to look at him. "Maybe the fact that one of the three other men standing there named Micah yelled at Whiskey for killing Baily. Whiskey told him to shut his mouth. That Raven would never know what happened because they would dump his body where the wild hogs would take care of him. That there would be nothing left to implicate anyone in his disappearance."

"What did you do then?"

"I got the hell out of town and I've been running ever since," Melora explained. "I do know how to take care of myself. I've been doing it for a while now."

"Sweetheart, I don't think you can outrun this, not if he keeps coming after you." He paused, then asked, "If you left town right after the murder, how did he know what you saw?"

Melora gritted her teeth. "I don't know for sure but I called the bar where I worked the next day and spoke to the bartender about leaving. She wasn't happy about it and told me Whiskey was sitting there. I hung up then but when I called her again a few days later, she told me Whiskey heard the conversation and knew there was a witness. He beat the hell out of her to find out where I was. She took it for a while but ended up telling him everything."

"Who did he kill?"

"A man name Baily Walker."

Sam raised his eyebrows. "Senator Walker's kid?"

"No, his nephew. He still wants to find him. I watched a news report just last week and he's now offering a reward for information on Baily's whereabouts."

"Someone like Walker isn't going to let it go without knowing the truth," Sam commented. He got to his feet and held out his hand, "Come on we have to go talk to my kid. He's the President of the local MC, Sin's Bastards. He can put a call into Raven and let him know what's going on."

Melora backed away from him like his hands were on fire. "Are you fucking nuts? If Raven knows there was a witness, he'll send his boys here to kill me. I won't have to wait for Whiskey to find me."

Sam narrowed his eyes at her. "If Raven didn't order the hit then Whiskey is the one to be worried. He killed the man, not you."

"That won't matter, not to the Ghosts," she insisted. "They'll still come after me. Right now, I only have four assholes to watch out for, if Raven finds out I'll have too many to watch for and one of them will get to me before I can get away." Shaking her head she murmured, "That's suicide and I'm not that crazy."

"No you'd rather run for the rest of your damned life." Sam growled. "One day, you'll run out of time and he'll find you. Then where will you be?"

"Then I'll die under Whiskey's blade but that day won't be today."

"Whiskey's blade?"

"Whiskey has this wicked knife he likes to show off and he knows very well how to use it." She shook her head. "A bullet would be quicker but he enjoys torturing his victims. He gets off on inflicting pain and all the blood. It's not a good way to die."

"Then we need to talk to Raven and get the record put right before this Whiskey finds you."

"You can tell him. Me? I'm leaving town while I still can."

"It's time to stop running."

Melora flushed. "I can't. If I stop—I'll die and I'm not ready to die just yet. I'm only twenty four. I'd like to live a longer life than that."

"Just talk to Deke. He can protect you while we figure this out."

"You can't promise me that, old man. I'm nothing to you or him. Raven might be President of the Ghosts but he's not here is he? He's several states away and Whiskey probably isn't."

"You need the protection of the MC," he insisted.

"No, I need to get the hell out of Dodge." Melora went over to the door and grabbed her coat. Turning to look at him she asked, "Are you going to give me a ride back or do I walk? Because I can do either."

"Get in the fucking truck." He growled, grabbing his own jacket.

Melora walked over to the truck and opened the door.

Sam joined her and without another word, he started the engine. A few minutes later, he spun the tires and drove down the driveway.

Entering the city, Melora kept watch, as they got closer to the shop. When Sam didn't pull into the driveway for the shop, she turned her head and glared at him. "You didn't stop."

"You're right, I didn't. You need to talk to Deke."

When she reached for the door handle, he grabbed her wrist. "I wouldn't suggest you jump from a moving vehicle. Your body won't appreciate it."

"I don't want to talk to Deke. I just want to leave town, why can't you understand that, old man?"

He hauled her closer to him. "You gave me more than just your body last night and again this morning. You gave me the right to protect you and this is me...protecting you. You're going to talk to Deke and let him handle this."

Melora glared at him. "God, I hate you right now. I didn't give you the rights you claim. All I did was share myself with you. I guess I should have stayed away."

Sam pulled into the parking lot of a strip club called Dirty Dancing.

Melora stared at the sign and snorted. "It figures."

"Don't judge until you know the facts darlin'." Sam muttered. "The girls who work here are just earning a living." Grasping her wrist, he dragged her into the club. He halted the striding in front of the bar top as he paused to gaze at the bartender.

The man nodded toward the back.

Sam then pulled her to an office. Barely knocking, he opened the door and pulled her inside.

A large, very good looking man sitting behind a huge desk looked up and found Sam staring at him. Frowning, he asked, "What's up?"

"We have a problem."

Deke looked beyond his father and found Melora glaring at the back of Sam's head. Throwing his pen down on the desk, he grumbled, "I don't have time for this shit."

"Make the time boy, this is life or death."

"What the fuck have you been doing, Bones?" Staring at the woman behind him again, he asked, "Isn't she a little young for you?"

Chapter Four

"Don't be a wiseass," Sam swore. "We may have visitors very soon. Visitors we don't want and certainly don't need."

"Visitors like who? And why would they come here?" Deke asked.

"One to four members of the Ghosts of Dixie MC and they're looking for her."

Deke sat up and studied Melora. "Why would they be after her?"

"They are looking to kill her to shut off a threat." Sam nodded at her. "She witnessed one of them committing murder and they've been chasing after her for two years."

Deke snorted. "Either she's very good or they are very bad at locating a witness. I can't imagine Raven letting this go for that long a time."

"Raven knows nothing about this woman," Sam explained. "He never ordered the hit she witnessed either. Apparently, he doesn't know what's going on in his own fuckin club."

"How did that happen?" he asked, staring at her even harder. "Suppose you sit down and tell me about this."

"I'd rather not," Melora retorted. "I told Sam I'd just leave town. Whiskey will follow and you'll never know either of us were here. He won't start trouble unless there's no other choice."

"Sam brought you here for a reason." Deke sat back in his chair. "I'd like to find out more about it before I commit to anything, and that includes letting you run."

"Neither of you have any right to stick your nose into my business," Melora told them.

"My father doesn't think so," Deke reminded her.

"Yeah, I know what the old man thinks, he made his opinion very clear this morning." She scoffed. "Only problem is I don't agree with him on that point."

"Yeah, well he's a stubborn sonofabitch sometimes." Deke chuckled.

"Will the two of you kindly not talk about me as if I'm not standing right here?" Sam grumbled.

"Cranky too, isn't he?" Melora shrugged.

"Cranky is about to paddle your ass again," Sam threatened.

Deke stared at his father for a moment then turned to her. "Why don't you tell me what you saw?"

Melora sighed heavily. "I don't really want to bring you guys into this."

"Tell him," Sam ordered.

She glared at him for a moment then turned to Deke. "September 10th two years ago I was living and working in Raleigh. It was close to one in the morning and I was outside having a smoke break when the door to the bar opened and five men came out. One man was a civilian named Baily Walker and the other four were members of the local MC, the Ghosts of Dixie. Apparently, Baily was in some kind of trouble with one of the men named Whiskey. Whiskey is a badass and he likes to hurt people. The four of them surrounded Baily and began punching him.' Melora paused with a sigh as she shook her head.

"Go on," Deke urged.

Melora frowned at Sam as she continued, "Whiskey was high that night, I could hear it in his voice. Whiskey being high makes him not only dangerous but mean too. That night he was mean. Whiskey pulled his knife out. He's known for that damn knife all over town. Everyone knows he loves to carve up people with it. He started carving on Baily. Baily screamed bloody hell but Whiskey didn't stop. Finally, he shoved the knife in his chest and Baily dropped to the ground. The other men with him started yelling at Whiskey. Telling him that Raven wasn't gonna like the fact that he'd killed Baily. In fact, Baily was supposed to be protected by Raven, so this wouldn't sit well at all. Whiskey told them it didn't matter because no one would ever find his body. They could take him out in the woods and let the wild hogs take care of him. No one would ever know what happened. They loaded his body up in a truck and drove away. Me? I got the hell out of town."

"Why was Raven protecting Baily?" Deke wanted to know.

"Baily was Senator Walker's nephew and Raven wanted a political connection, even if it was one under the table."

Deke ran his fingers through his hair. "Fuck a duck." He got to his feet and began to pace behind the desk. Then he looked at Melora. "Did anyone ever find Baily's body?"

"I doubt it, wild hogs will eat anything and they don't usually leave parts behind."

"So you don't have any evidence that this ever happened?"

Melora shrugged. "Well, I never said that."

Both Sam and Deke snapped their heads around to stare at her.

She shrugged. "Well, no one ever asked me that before."

"What evidence do you have?" Deke asked.

"I videoed the whole thing with my smartphone, once I figured out what was going on."

"Why didn't you send the video to Raven?" Deke asked.

"Cuz I ain't stupid." Melora snorted. "I may have seen those guys around town but I didn't know them personally. My momma didn't raise no fool."

"Where have you been staying since you got to town?" Deke asked.

"She's been staying in the warehouse at the back of the shop," Sam answered.

"Okay, we'll get your things and move you to the compound while I contact Raven."

"Boy, you guys just don't quit do you?" Melora got to her feet. "I told you already I'm not staying!" She began to pace. "I heard Whiskey's bike in town the other day and I ain't sticking around where he can find me."

Deke got to his feet and glared at her from across his desk. "What you don't understand is the fact you aren't going anywhere until this is settled. I'm not going to turn you out into the streets and watch this Whiskey character kill you or allow you to bring a war to the streets of my town. That just ain't happening, little girl."

Melora growled. "I can take care of myself. I am not a little girl. What is it with you bikers? I've been taking care of myself since I was a kid. I don't need you or the old man to pat me on the head and tell me to let you take care of things."

"Then why are you still on the run after two years?" Deke asked. "Why haven't you just killed this Whiskey guy and his friends?"

Before she could answer him, a knock came to the door.

Deke turned and waited until the door opened.

It was Wiley. "Boss we might have a situation."

"What kind of situation?"

"Well, Iceman just called and said he saw three men wearing different colors riding into town. Said they were Ghosts of Dixie brothers. Then Gator called and said he just had a call from a man named Mountain asking for a parley with you."

"Who the hell is Mountain?"

Wiley shook his head and replied, "He hails from a little town in Texas and he says he's looking for someone. He and his party are Los Hijos de Diablo, the Sons of Satan. " He paused then added, "I've heard of this club and it's not one you want to mess with if you don't have to."

Deke turned to observe Melora for a moment then turned to Wiley. "I need you to go to the warehouse behind the shop and collect the things inside. Bring them out to the compound but try not to let anyone see you there. I'm calling everyone in for a meeting. I want a show of power when this Mountain gets there. Did Gator say how many were with this guy?"

Wiley nodded. "Yeah, Mountain said he had a party of ten with him. He also said to tell you, he didn't want any trouble, he just wanted our help."

Deke wondered what the other man wanted but he needed to get the girl back first. He couldn't take any chances on getting caught out in the open until he talked to Raven and cleared things up with him. "Start the calling tree and we'll meet at the clubhouse. Collect her things first and bring them with you. I want no sign of her at the warehouse in case Whiskey or the other Ghosts can find where she's been staying."

Sam walked over to Melora and grasped her by the arm. "Come on darlin' let's get you under wraps till we can figure this out." He turned to Deke. "I'll take her to the compound and meet you back there."

Deke nodded. "Let's hope nothing happens until after we talk to Raven."

~****~

Twenty minutes later, Deke met them back at the compound. The compound was on lockdown until after the meeting with the man named Mountain. They didn't know what or who he was after but Deke didn't want trouble.

Everyone was still gathering but there were enough of them here to let them in, to parley.

Deke and Gator sat at the head table, their guns in front of them. Iceman and Sam were sitting at different tables but they were both watching. Deke made eye contact with his father and noted the woman Melora was sitting next to him.

She kept her head down and wasn't looking at anyone. It seemed almost as if she didn't want any attention.

This behavior made Deke curious about what else she might be hiding.

The entire room went silent as Wiley led the members of Los Hijos de Diablo inside.

The lead man was huge, at least six foot eight and close to four hundred pounds. He wasn't a fat man, all his body weight was pure muscle. His hair was long and a startling white, caught back in a ponytail, it hung well past his shoulder blades. He wore sunglasses atop his head. He was dressed in jeans and a red t-shirt under his leather jacket, heavy boots and his club's cut.

It was only when he got closer, Deke could see the unusual color of his eyes. They were almost violet, not blue or green or brown but violet. He froze and glanced over the girl beside his father.

She still didn't look up.

What the hell was going on here? Deke knew there was more here than met the eye, so to speak.

The patch on his cut said he was President of his club and he walked confidently to the table where Deke and Gator sat. His men took position behind him but they made no movement that could be taken as aggressive. They simply stood there waiting. He could see they were all armed but their hands hung down at their sides.

Deke got to his feet and held out his hand.

Mountain shook it then sat down.

Deke poured them a drink.

Mountain took the glass and tipped it down his throat.

Deke did the same and then asked, "So tell me, what brings you guys all the way to New York?" Deke asked. "I understand you hail from Texas."

Mountain nodded. "Our chapter is from Sabine Pass, actually. It's a small town on the Texas/ Louisiana border." He tipped his glass on the table and circled it before he spoke again, "I'm actually looking for someone who may be in your area."

"And who would that be?"

"My kid," Mountain admitted. "Actually, I'm not real sure where she is, so I'm reaching out to the MC brotherhood to help me find her."

"I don't understand."

Mountain sighed. "Up until four years ago, I didn't know I even had a kid, then some lawyer from Chicago got in touch with me and told me I had a daughter. In a letter, my ex- girlfriend sent gave me proof the girl was mine. Her mother said that if I ever got the letter she was dead and she was hoping I would reach out and find my daughter. The lawyer said she went through the foster system but she took off eight years ago when she was sixteen. He also said no one had seen her since then. I was able to find her trail and track her as far as North Carolina but lost her two years ago. Haven't had any word since then, so I'm going through the clubs in the area to see if they can help me find her."

~ * * * *~

When Sam heard Mountain's story, he turned and stared at Melora.

She wouldn't look at him or anyone else in the room. Her face was frozen but it showed no emotion at all.

He turned back to the main table and watched as Deke and Mountain talked softly.

"Why did your old lady wait so long to tell you about your kid?" Deke asked.

"She didn't know where I was," he explained. "We were only together for a short time, something like a week. She didn't know how to contact me and it took several years after she died for the lawyer to find me."

"Do you know what your daughter looks like?" Deke finally asked after a long moment of silence.

Mountain reached inside his cut and pulled out a photo. "This is an old photo and she's only a kid but she can't have changed much." He handed the photo over to Deke.

It showed a small kid with her dad's white hair and violet eyes. She was small and thin. The picture was taken in a park somewhere but it was hard to say exactly where the park was. It didn't show anything else and there was no one else in the small picture.

"This could be anyone," Deke noted. "Does she have any scars or birthmarks?"

"The attorney told me she got a tattoo when she was sixteen and still in foster care. She had to lie about her age but she got a small pink rose on her left shoulder." He shrugged. "I was lead to believe she left the system shortly after that and was living on the streets since then. The attorney didn't know where she was but someone from my club found her trail over the years. I was able to track her movement at least for a little while. Then I lost her again, two years ago, as I said earlier."

"What's her name?"

"Her birth certificate says it's Merry Loran Shaw. I'm not sure what name she goes by now."

"How long are you guys in town for in case we do see her?"

"We'll be here for another three days." Mountain shook his head. "I hope I can find her soon. I know she may not want to find me but I just need the chance to know her, even if it's only for a short time. I just need to know she's all right."

"Where can we reach you if we find her?" Deke asked as he got to his feet.

Mountain stood and passed him a card. "You can reach me at that phone number any time. We have to go home pretty soon but I can come back if I need to. Like I said before, I'm not looking to start any kind of trouble I just want to find my kid. I would appreciate any help you could give me."

His men turned and began to walk toward the door when one of them turned his head and caught Melora's eyes. He gasped and cocked his head to study her. She was staring at Mountain and wasn't paying attention to anyone else. It was by accident the other man saw her at all. He stopped and stared at her.

When Mountain turned, he saw his man staring at someone a few tables down. Turning his head, he caught the stare of the young woman sitting there. His eyes narrowed as he stared at her. Then Mountain changed his course and began walking toward her.

Melora lowered her face but Mountain kept coming toward her. He stopped in front of her and leaned closer. Reaching out, he lifted her face to his and stared at her. Violet eyes met violet eyes and Mountain searched her face for something familiar he might recognize in her.

Then he reached out and pushed her shirt off her shoulder. When he could see the small pink rose on her skin he whispered, "Merry?"

Melora closed her eyes and shook her head slightly. She refused to say anything.

Sam got to his feet and laid a hand on her shoulder.

Mountain turned to stare at the older man. Neither of them said a word and eventually, Mountain turned and began walking toward the front door. His men fell in line behind him.

It was only when they were gone that anyone moved. Sam grabbed her arm and hauled her to her feet.

Deke, Gator and Iceman led the way while Sam and Melora followed them back to Deke's office.

Only when the door closed behind them did Deke speak, "So who exactly are you?"

Melora shrugged. "My name is Melora."

"Let me rephrase that, what name did your mother give you when you were born?"

"I think you know," she whispered, still not looking at anyone in the room.

"You had white hair as a child."

"Still do," Melora admitted. Reaching up she took the wig off and her natural hair fell out. Her braid fell down her back and everyone was stunned to see how long it was. It fell almost to the floor. It looked like light blonde silk.

The men in the room all stared at her for a long silent moment.

"Why didn't you step forward when he was still here?" Sam asked as he stared at her hair.

Melora glared at him. "I don't know that man from Adam and I've learned many hard lessons about keeping my identity to myself." She grabbed the wig and began stuffing her long silky strands back up into it.

"I hardly think he's looking to hurt you," Iceman stated. "He just wants to find you."

"You all heard what he said as clear as I did," Melora argued. "He only knew my mother about a week, what makes you think he wants to know me at all? I'm nothing to him."

"He says he's been looking for you for four years," Deke reminded her.

"Yeah, and it took a lawyer a hell of a lot longer to find him." Melora scoffed. "My mother died when I was ten. Where the hell was he for those missing ten years?"

"You could always ask him," Sam suggested.

"I don't really care one way or the other." She shrugged. "It was his choice to leave my mother all those years ago, now he can just stay gone. I don't need him or want him in my life. I've been alone for a while now and that suits me just fine."

"He's your father," Deke stated quietly.

Melora hung her head and shook it. "No he's just a man that screwed my mom at the right time for me to be born nine months later. He didn't stick around then, and I don't need him in my life now." She turned and walked away, closing the door behind her.

After a few minutes, Gator commented, "Well, that went well, don't you think?"

Deke pushed his fingers through his hair. "I don't think we've seen the last of him, do you?"

Sam snorted. "Not likely. He knows she's here now and I don't think he's leaving just yet."

"Would you?" Gator asked. "Could you really walk away from a kid you never knew existed if you finally found her after four long years of looking for her?"

"Not fuckin likely." Iceman growled. Looking over at Deke he asked, "So what are you going to do about this?"

Deke barked a laugh. "You don't know what else is going on here man. That girl is running from four members of the Ghosts of Dixie. One of whom is a murderer and is looking for her to kill her."

"Are you fuckin serious?" Iceman asked.

Chapter Five

"Dead serious," Deke admitted. "The only problem is Raven doesn't know about it, or at least I don't think he does."

"This girl is nothing but trouble," Iceman argued. "Do we really need this kind of headache right now?"

"No but we don't have a choice," Deke replied. "I can't turn a kid like her out on the streets with the problems she has. Cassie would kill me."

Iceman winced. "I hear that, Peaches would do the same to me."

Gator shook his head with a smile. "Damn Bones..." He looked over at Sam. "...When trouble looks for you, it lands big, don't it?"

Sam grunted and gave him a glare but he mostly ignored his old friend. Then he disappeared for a moment and when he came back, he brought Melora with him. "We all need to understand what's going on here." He held her hand, so she would have no choice but to stay.

"What is this evidence you told us about?" Deke asked her.

Melora glared at him then brought out her phone. She flipped through the buttons and found the video she was looking for. Then she handed it to Deke.

All four men gathered around as he hit the play button. She had indeed caught Baily's murder on video. Not only the murder but the conversation afterwards, all the way to the moment the truck turned the corner and the street was empty.

"So who was this kid?" Iceman asked in the silence that followed.

"Senator Walker's nephew," Deke replied. "He was under Raven's protection and no one knows what happened to him. Walker has been looking for him since he disappeared two years ago."

"Damn." Iceman swore. "You have to call Raven and clue him in."

"Yeah I do, but if that happens he's gonna send a posse after Whiskey and his boys and then we'll have a war in our streets." Deke countered.

"He has to know."

"I know." Deke ran his hand over his face. Then he glanced over at Melora. "And you aren't going anywhere until this is settled. I'm not risking anyone's life over you."

"I never asked to be here," Melora protested. "I didn't want to put anyone between me and Whiskey." She turned and glared at Sam. "He's the one who brought me here against my will. Just let me go and Whiskey's bullshit won't come down on you or this club."

Deke ignored her outburst and stared at Sam. "You brought her in, you keep track of her, twenty four seven."

Sam nodded. "I can do that."

"You'd better. Try not to lose her until this is over or it will be your blood that's spilled." Deke reached for the phone. He nodded at the door and everyone left him alone to make the call to Raven.

~* * * *~

Sam grabbed her hand and dragged her back to the bedroom they would share. As he closed the door behind them, he flipped the lock and put the key in his pocket.

Melora paced back and forth in front of the bed. "This is exactly why I didn't want to come here."

"Why is that darlin'?" Sam asked casually as he went over to the bed and stretched out.

"Your son is risking his life and those of his club to keep Whiskey out. Whiskey is plain crazy. He isn't going to let anyone stand between me and certain death at his hands. He has to kill me now."

"Honey, he's always had to kill you...you just didn't know it at the time," he assured her. Sam patted the bed and urged her to sit down beside him. When she did, he continued, "He doesn't know where you are yet. Hopefully, we'll be able to neutralize him before he knows where to find you."

"It hasn't worked out that way in the past, why should it now?"

Sam frowned. "How did he find you before?"

Melora shrugged. "I have no idea. When I left Raleigh, I didn't tell anyone where I was going. Hell, I didn't know myself. I did call a friend to tell her I would be out of town and I asked her to collect my last paycheck."

"Could he have known you would call her?"

Melora shrugged. "I don't think he would have. The only one who even knew we were friends was another bartender at the club I worked in. Gloria wouldn't have told him anything."

"Not even if he forced her too?"

Melora paled. "Maybe? I did call her after I left town. I asked her to let Izzy collect my check."

"Who's Izzy?"

"She's the only friend I have in the world," Melora admitted. "She's the only one I've kept in touch with since I left Raleigh."

Sam snapped his fingers. "I'll bet Whiskey knows this Izzy. He'd have to in order to keep track of you all this time. Izzy has been telling him where you are every time you call."

Melora shook her head. "Izzy wouldn't do that."

"Honey, she may not have had a choice. If Whiskey is desperate to find you, he would use whoever he could."

Melora flopped down on the bed. "Damn his ornery hide."

Sam began undressing and when he was naked, he pulled her up and around to lay next to him. "There isn't anything more we can do tonight, so let's get some rest. Things may not seem so desperate in the morning."

"No it will probably be worse," she muttered. She sat up and loosened her braid. Shaking her fingers through her hair, she groaned.

Sam was entranced by those long silken strands. "Your hair is beautiful but why do you hide it under a wig?"

"It makes people remember me," she answered simply. "I can't be hidden from the world if people remember me."

"I've never seen anyone with hair so long or so light." He reached out to smooth his fingers along it. "Like silk…"

"My mom told me once that a woman's hair was her crowning glory. Her hair was down to her ass. I've never cut it in memory of her. It kept me connected to her even after her death."

Sam pushed her on her back and leaned over her. He pulled her top off. His mouth touched hers…then something changed and his kiss went from warm to very hot within seconds. His hands ran up and down her sides, finally settling on her breasts. He slipped her bra straps down then reached behind her and unsnapped it, throwing the bra to the floor. His hands kneaded her breasts then thumbing her nipples, Sam kissed a path to her chest. Taking one nipple into his mouth he bit down on it gently and Melora squirmed under him. Pinching the other nipple between his fingers, she whimpered. Lifting her ass off the bed, he pulled her jeans and underwear off.

She opened her legs and exposed her core.

Accepting the sexy offering, he reached down and he rammed two fingers deep inside her.

Melora moaned and raised her hips to meet his fingers. Over and over he dipped inside her. Harder and deeper he rammed them in. Melora reached out, grabbed his cock and fisted it. Each stroke with her hands brought him closer to where he wanted to be. Finally, he couldn't stand it anymore and he settled between her legs. As he rammed himself inside her, they both groaned.

"Harder…" She moaned. "…I need you harder. I'm so close. Please…"

Sam ramped up and soon was lost as he stroked harder and faster. He could feel her responding and that made him ready to blow. Then it hit them both. Melora cried out and Sam stiffened as they both climaxed together. Sweat beaded Sam's forehead and dripped down to Melora but neither of them cared. Melora closed her eyes and tears spilled down her cheeks.

Sam saw them and rolled beside her. "What's wrong? Did I hurt you? I mean I know I'm kind of rough."

Melora shook her head. Turning, she looked at him. "No you didn't hurt me," she whispered. "I'm just wondering why you are the only man I've ever wanted to sleep with?"

Sam chuckled. "I have no fucking clue but I'm glad to hear that."

"Why is that?"

"Because I'm a possessive old man. As long as we're together, you won't be allowed to stray. I'll kill anyone who tries to touch you."

"And how long will that be?"

"As long as both of us want it or until I get tired of it," Sam admitted. "But I don't think that's gonna happen anytime soon."

"I can't promise anything as long as Whiskey is out there," Melora warned. "I may not want to leave but may not have a choice. I won't risk anyone else's life." She paused then whispered, "For some reason, I feel safe here with you and I haven't felt that way in a long time."

"You won't risk your life either." Sam's arms wrapped around her and held her close. "You're safe here and no one will hurt you behind these walls."

Melora was tired of the fight and of living in fear so she didn't object. She snuggled into Sam's embrace and closed her eyes. "Whatever you say old man, whatever you say. Now be quiet, I'm going to sleep."

Sam grinned as he snuggled down beside her. He kept stroking her silky hair and for the first time in his life, he was in awe of something...Someone.

~****~

A few hours later, three motorcycles roared up to the main gate. Mountain and two of his men sat aboard them.

Wiley was making rounds and came up to the front gate.

"I need to talk to Deke and the girl." Mountain barked. "I can't wait till daylight."

"Wait here." Wiley told him. He turned and walked around behind the clubhouse. Fifteen minutes later Wiley came back, Deke was there as well.

Mountain was leaning up against his bike waiting. "I want to talk to the girl again."

"It's the middle of the night man, can't you wait until it's light out?"

Mountain shook his head. "I need to know if she's my kid." He waited and when Deke didn't say anything Mountain asked, "Would you wait until daylight if your kid might be inside these walls?"

Deke sighed then reached over and hit the code to unlock the gate.

Mountain threw his leg over his bike and rode up to the door of the clubhouse. His men followed,

Wiley shut the gate and locked it after they were inside.

Mountain watched as Deke walked up to the doorway. Opening it, he allowed the three men inside. Snapping on the lights Deke went to the kitchen and made a pot of coffee.

When he joined the others in the main room, he sat down and motioned for them to sit. Looking at Mountain, he asked, "What are you going to do if this girl is your daughter?"

"Fair question." Mountain nodded. "All I want to know is that she's all right and if she needs anything. I'm not here to start trouble but I do want to know her."

"Can I ask a question?" one of Mountain's men asked.

Deke turned and stared at him. "What do you want to know?"

"Why is this compound on lockdown?"

"Because the girl you came here to find is being hunted."

Mountain stiffened. "By who and for what?" he sneered.

Deke sighed and rubbed his hands over his face. "Two years ago, she witnessed a murder. A member of the Ghosts of Dixie knifed a man under Raven's protection then hid the murder. He knows she saw what he did and he's been after her ever since."

"Raven knows this and allows it to happen?" Mountain asked. "That doesn't sound like Raven."

Deke glanced over at Mountain. "You know Raven?"

Mountain nodded. "We've done business in the past."

"Do you know any of his crew?"

Mountain shrugged. "Some but not all."

"Do you know a man named Whiskey?"

Mountain and the others grunted with disgust. "Yeah, we know the bastard. Why?"

"He's the one after the girl," Deke informed him.

Mountain sighed heavily. "Now why doesn't that surprise me?" He rubbed his hands across the back of his neck. "Who was it Whiskey murdered?"

"Senator Walkers' nephew Baily."

One of the men with Mountain snorted again. "Whiskey always was a stupid little shit."

"That's gonna kill Raven's political connection. Why would he do that?" Mountain asked.

"I don't think Raven ordered the hit," Deke replied. "In fact, Baily was under his protection."

No one said anything for a moment. Then Mountain asked, "Is there any proof? Raven isn't gonna take some chick's word for what happened. He's gonna want proof."

"Yeah, there's proof. The girl recorded the whole thing."

Mountain sat there a moment then smoothed his hand along his chin. "Can I see this proof?"

Deke took Melora's phone out of his pocket and played the video for him.

Mountain didn't say anything for a minute then reached for his own phone. He waited until someone answered then asked to speak to Raven.

While he spoke to Raven, Deke got up and went to get the coffee. When he got back, Mountain was done with his conversation.

When Deke poured the coffee, Mountain told him, "I asked Raven to come up here. He needs to see the video and handle Whiskey himself."

"That's just what Melora didn't want," Deke told him. "She didn't want to start a war with another club."

"This won't start a war," Mountain declared. "Raven needs to know the truth. He needs to know what's going on in his own club. He had no idea what happened to Baily and he was pissed when I told him."

"I agree with you on that point." Deke nodded. "But I won't turn her over to him or to you if she doesn't want to go."

Mountain stared at him for a long minute. "Message understood but I need to know if she's my kid."

Deke nodded and got to his feet. He went down the hall to his old bedroom and knocked on the door. When his dad answered, he passed along the message and went back to his table. "Sam will be out in a minute."

"Who is he? Is that the older guy who was sitting next to the girl?" Mountain asked.

Deke nodded. "He brought her in."

"What do you know about her?"

"She claims her name is Melora and she's been running for two years now." Deke shrugged. "That's about all I know. Maybe Sam knows more but the girl doesn't like to talk about her life."

Sam joined them a moment later. He sat and stared at Mountain.

No one said a word and when the door to the bedroom opened up again, everyone turned to stare at her.

Melora came out of the bedroom dressed but nothing covered her pale, silken hair. Her white locks flowed around her all the way to the floor. She walked out staring into Mountain's eyes. She heard him gasp but she didn't smile. Finally, she sat down next to Sam and reached for his hand. Staring at her father, she told him, "My name is Merry Loran Shaw."

Chapter Six

Mountain took his time looking her over. Her pale hair shimmered in the light. "Are you Carla's daughter?"

Melora nodded. She wasn't going to make this easy for him.

"Why didn't you speak up before?" Mountain wanted to know.

"You were just the man that screwed my mother twenty four years ago. I don't owe you anything nor do I want anything from you. My mother gave me everything she had, everything I needed. You, I don't even know. What's more important, you don't know me either."

"I didn't know you because Carla never told me you were born," Mountain argued. "How can you hold that against me?"

"She gave you everything she had for seven days and you never came back." Melora scoffed. "Did you know she waited for you for ten years? Did you know she never found anyone else to care about her after you left? She died still loving you."

Mountain hung his head. When he lifted it, she could see his eyes were swimming in tears but they never fell. "The hardest thing I ever did in my entire life was to ride away from her that day. I never found another woman who could take her place in my heart, but it never occurred to me that she was waiting for me to come back for her."

"She once told me she loved a lifetime in that week you were together," Melora whispered. "She tried to find you after I was born but she didn't know anything about you."

"Oh, she knew about me." Mountain nodded. "She named you after my mother and her grandmother. Merry was your great-grandmothers' name, Loran was my mother's name. She remembered that much."

"She remembered more than that," Melora admitted. "She used to tell me stories about you, little things the two of you did while you were with her. The only thing she didn't tell me was your name. She would never tell me who you were."

"My name is Talon Morgan. My club name is Mountain because I'm so big. My family lives in Iowa. I have a father and four brothers there. My club family is from Sabine Pass, Texas. That's where I ended up after I left her and you in Chicago. I've been there for twenty four years and that's where I'll die. It's a good place to live and I'm hoping you'll come back there with me."

Melora shook her head. "I can't do that."

"Why not?"

"I'm in trouble with another club and if they find me, they will kill me." Melora explained. Looking around she added, "I didn't want to come here but Sam here didn't give me a choice."

Mountain turned to stare at Sam. He noted the fact of how he had moved closer to her after she sat down and they both came out of the same bedroom. He also saw Sam's hand on her shoulder and knowing she was his daughter this bothered Mountain. "How long have you been with the old man?"

Sam stiffened at the tone of his voice.

Melora laid her hand on Sam's. "I met him two days ago."

"Isn't that a little soon to be sleeping with him?" Mountain asked.

Melora sneered. "You got no say in how I live my life or who I sleep with. As far as I'm concerned you're just a donor."

"I'm your father." Mountain growled as his hands tightened in fists.

Melora shook her head. "My mother may have loved you but you weren't there for either of us. We may share the same blood but you weren't there to be my father when I needed one and you can scream it from the tops of the mountains but it doesn't make you my father."

Mountain paled and stared at her. "Your mother never told me about you, how can you blame me for that?"

"You walked away from us a long time ago. Apparently, you meant more to her than she did to you." She got to her feet. "You found me, I don't need or want anything from you, so you're free to go home and live your life anyway you choose."

"I want to know you. I want to know what kind of woman you've become. Is that too much to ask?" Mountain seethed. "You're my daughter."

Melora coldly gazed at him. "No it isn't too much to ask. I often wondered what kind of man you were too. But there is a crazy man after me and he's looking to kill me to keep his fucking secret. I won't put anyone's life in danger to save my own."

"Whiskey isn't going to get close enough to you to hurt you," Mountain assured her.

Melora snapped her head to glare at Deke. Turning back to her father she stated, "He won't let you stand between him and what he wants. He's crazy enough to think he can't be stopped."

"Raven will stop him."

"Raven isn't here and has no fucking clue what Whiskey is about!" Melora yelled.

"He's on his way and he will know when he gets here what Whiskey has done," Mountain assured her. "Deke showed me the video."

Melora curled her fingers into fists. Turning toward Deke she screamed, "Are you all fucking nuts? Why don't you take out a billboard ad? Sweet Jesus!" She hung her head for a moment then added, "You don't know how desperate Whiskey is getting. He's not afraid of anything anymore and that makes him dangerous. The last time I saw him he was so stoned, he didn't even know where he was. Even the two men with him looked nervous, just being there with him."

"How did you figure he was stoned?" Mountain's man asked.

"I've seen stoned before. I may not use drugs but I know what a person looks like who's under the influence. I've seen Whiskey enough to know what he looks like when he's high. He's beyond that. He's out of control."

"Then he'll make a mistake and he'll be done," Deke stated in a cold tone. "My wife and children are here and I'll not put their lives in danger. My brothers live here as well and I won't put their lives or those of their families on the line either. Whiskey will not get through our defenses."

Sam drew her back to his lap. When she settled, he wrapped his arms around her. "You have to trust us. We can keep you safe."

Melora laid her head on his shoulder and closed her eyes. She was so tired of running, so tired of being afraid. "I need some sleep. I'm going back to bed. Are you coming?"

~* * * *~

Melora didn't see Mountain clenching his hands into fists and that he glared at the older man.

Although, Sam did see Mountain's reaction. He kissed her temple and said, "You go ahead. I want to talk to Deke first."

Melora got to her feet and went back to the bedroom.

After she closed the door, Sam turned to Mountain. "What do you have to say to me?"

"Stay away from my daughter. She's young enough to be your kid." He growled.

Sam nodded. "True enough, she is. But you heard her, she doesn't think of you as her father."

"Dad, maybe you should give the girl some room for the moment," Deke suggested.

"I won't abandon her now or ever," Sam argued. "She needs someone on her side right now and that's gonna be me."

"I want the time with her to get to know me as her father. I didn't get that chance before now but I want it," Mountain announced firmly.

"You can have that time but I'm going to be there in her corner too, whether you want me there or not. I will not abandon her. Get used to it." Sam got to his feet and walked the short way to the bedroom door.

~* * * *~

Mountain glared at the closed door but didn't move from his chair. Instead, he sat there and curled his fingers into fists.

Deke got up and walked over to the bar. Grabbing a bottle of whiskey and some glasses, he went back to where Mountain sat. Pouring each man a glass, he set the bottle down and lifted the liquor to his lips.

Mountain and the others slammed their drinks down.

"So who are your men?" Deke asked, pointing to the other two men.

"Chase and Rigger," Mountain replied.

Deke poured another round.

Chase got up and went over to the wall where Cassie's paintings were.

Deke turned his head and told him, "The tiger is Rufus and the lion is Diablo. My wife is the artist."

"She's good," Chase commented with awe in his voice.

Deke smiled briefly, then turned back to Mountain. "So was meeting your daughter everything you wanted it to be?"

"Your dad isn't helping." Mountain sneered.

Deke nodded as he drank another round. "Yeah, he's good like that. The old bastard never did what was right, he only did what was right *for* him. Never took anyone else's wants and needs into consideration."

"Can't you order him to leave her alone?" Chase asked. "You are the president of this club."

"Yeah, I could do that," Deke admitted. "But then it would be Melora breaking the laws of the club. She wants him near her. If she has to break the rules, she's gonna be pissed and that won't endear Mountain to her, now would it? She might just do it for spite and he won't want that either."

"He's right," Mountain agreed. "I wish to Christ he wasn't but he is. I need to know her and let her know me." He glanced over at Deke.

"The rest of our boys need to get behind the fence before Raven and his boys get here. Is that gonna be a problem?"

Deke shook his head. "No, we have room for them. I'd just as soon they got here before Whiskey finds out where she is though."

"They can be here within half an hour," Mountain assured him. Glancing over at Rigger, he nodded.

Rigger got on the phone and within twenty minutes, the other eight men were at the gate.

Wiley let them in and closed the gate behind them. As the men entered the Clubhouse, Mountain introduced them to Deke. "This is Elan, Jax, Doc, Pistol, Payne, Lance, Spirit and Blue."

"So is the girl your daughter?" Doc asked.

Mountain nodded. "But we have a bit of trouble. She's got a killer after her. We can't start a war but we can have some fun." He smiled.

"Who's the bastard after her?" Jax asked.

"Whiskey from the Ghosts of Dixie."

"Can we kill him this time?" Pistol asked.

Deke raised an eyebrow. "This time?"

"Yeah, we've run into Whiskey before," Mountain explained. "Raven stayed our hand before but I don't think that will be the case this time."

"Not once he sees the video." Rigger scoffed.

"Who's with him?" Pistol asked.

"Micah and Lightning."

"Oh, now that's too bad." Jax grinned.

Deke frowned. "What's going on here?"

Mountain turned to him and explained, "Like I said we've done business with Whiskey before and he's screwed us. He knew we couldn't touch him without starting a war Raven and I didn't want and for a while, he hid behind Raven's protection. Now I don't think that'll be a problem."

Deke got to his feet. "There are rooms in the back for you and your men. I'm going home to my wife. I'll see you in the morning."

Mountain held out his hand. "Thank you man."

Deke nodded as he shook his hand.

~* * * *~

The next morning, Reva and Gator came to the clubhouse and found Mountain sitting alone at a table nursing a cup of coffee. Reva went to the kitchen while Gator went to sit with the other man.

"So you came back?"

"She's my kid and she hates me," Mountain grumbled.

Gator shook his head. "She doesn't hate you, she just doesn't know you. She feels you ran out on her mom and left them alone for too long."

"She'd be right about that."

"So what are you gonna do about it?" Gator asked as he crossed his arms over his chest.

"What can I do?"

"You can show her what kind of man you really are. She doesn't know you right now. Let her in and show her what kind of man you want to be for her."

"She doesn't need a dad anymore," Mountain told him. "She's already made that fact very clear."

"She doesn't need a daddy, that's true. But she does need a father," Gator assured him.

Mountain stared at him. "Is there a difference?"

"There's a big difference. You just have to figure out what that might be."

Mountain snorted. "I also need to get her away from that old man."

Gator shook his head. "I wouldn't even try if I were you."

Mountain glared at him. "He's probably older than I am."

"I know but Bones is a force all his own. You tell him he can't have something and he'll fight you tooth and nail just to prove he can."

"How do you know?"

"I've known that bastard for many years, more than I care to count," Gator admitted.

"He's too old for her," Mountain muttered.

"She's a woman full grown, you can't tell her what to do or who she can see," Gator advised. "She's been through hell and back all on her own and she won't take kindly to anyone telling who she can be with now."

"How do you know what she's been through?"

"Deke had Zipper check her out," Gator explained. "He found out everything about her after you guys got here. After her mother died when she was ten, she lived in thirteen different foster homes in six years. Some of them weren't good places for a child to live. She took off and hid when she was sixteen. Life can be hard for kids sometimes. Most are lucky but there are a few who aren't. She managed to get by but it wasn't easy for her."

"Thirteen foster homes?" Mountain looked shaken. "I wish I'd known that. No wonder she hates me."

Gator shook his head. "I don't think she hates you. She just thinks she doesn't need you. It's up to you to prove to her that she does."

"What do you suggest I do?"

"Tell her little things about her mother that she doesn't know. Give her your memories of Carla. That's your connection."

Mountain thought about it and nodded. "I can do that."

"How long before Raven gets here?" Gator asked.

Mountain shrugged. "It's probably about a ten hour drive, give or take a bit. I called him at around one o'clock this morning, so he should be here sometime late morning."

"Ok, that's good. We need to get this matter with him and Whiskey settled."

Mountain grinned. "My boys are actually looking forward to battling Whiskey."

"Are they nuts?" Gator scoffed.

"No, they're looking for payback."

"What kind of payback?" Gator asked.

"Whiskey put one of our own in a wheelchair for the rest of his life. He waited until Travis was alone and ambushed him in an alley. Shot him in the back and left him there to die. My boys couldn't touch him that time, Raven wouldn't allow it. This time, it will be a different story."

"Maybe." Gator looked around. "But you have to remember one thing about Whiskey, he's getting desperate, and desperate men do crazy things to get by. He might figure he's got nothing left to lose."

"Ain't no maybe about it." Mountain narrowed his violet eyes. "Deke showed me the video and Raven is gonna be pissed when he sees it. Whiskey deliberately disobeyed orders and he showed no concern with Raven's wishes. That's gonna hurt him in the end."

The door to the bedroom Melora and Sam shared opened and Melora came out. She ignored Mountain and went straight to the kitchen. When she came back out, she sat down at the table and stared at the man claiming to be her father. Her hair was covered with a brown wig now and she seemed closed off to him. "Did you get any sleep last night?" she asked.

Mountain shook his head. "No I didn't."

"Why not?"

"Didn't need any." He shrugged. "I don't generally sleep much anyway. Too many fucking dreams and they aren't the good kind. I can catch a nap this afternoon."

Melora sat there staring at her coffee cup. "We met once, you know."

Mountain frowned. "When and where?"

"I was working in Shreveport for a while a couple of years back. I was a bartender at Reece's. You and your boys showed up one night."

"Why didn't you tell me who you were?"

Melora shrugged. "At first, I didn't know who you were. I was trying to remember everything my mom said about you and for the longest time, I couldn't remember anything. Then you laughed at something and I remembered her describing the way you laughed. It was exactly as she described. I had to wonder if everything she told me was true or not. For the longest time, I couldn't take my eyes off of you. Then all the sudden, I remembered everything my mom ever said about you."

"What did you think of me then?"

"I didn't know you." She paused. "I still don't."

Mountain sighed. "I wish I had known about you before then."

"You spoke to me that day," Melora admitted. "I almost revealed who I was. I really wanted to but then you just turned and walked away. I couldn't help but compare that to what my Mom said you did the day you left and never looked back."

"What did I say?"

"You told me I had the same colored eyes as you did and how seldom you found anyone with violet eyes." She licked her dry lips. "I was wearing a red wig that day and I really wanted to take it off and show you my hair."

"I wish you had. Maybe we would have found each other sooner."

"No." Melora shook her head. "I don't think either of us was ready for that yet. You had no reason to believe I was your daughter at that time."

"I knew shortly after leaving Chicago that I had just made the biggest mistake of my life."

"What mistake was that?" Melora asked.

"Leaving your mother behind."

"Why didn't you go back for her?"

"That's something I've asked myself for years but I never could answer it," Mountain admitted. "I wasn't ready to admit to myself I needed her in my life. Then when I knew I did…too much time had passed. I didn't think she'd remember anything about our time together and I wasn't going to humiliate myself by chasing her down."

"So you were scared?" Melora rolled her eyes.

"Yeah, I guess I was," he admitted. Running his fingers through his hair he told her, "I had just come back from my second tour in the war on terror. I was only twenty four years old. I was heart sick with the things I'd seen and done. All I wanted was to find a little peace. When I met Carla, I'd just begun my journey. I had a lot of things to work out but she gave me the first tiny bit of peace that started me healing. Both of us knew before we even got started that one day, I would just get on my bike and leave. She knew it but she gave herself to me anyway and for a short moment in time, I had everything I needed. She was sweet to me when I needed sweet I guess. She held me in her arms at night when the darkness came for me. She cried when I called out the names of my friends who wouldn't come home again. She just listened when I needed to talk. She was the one who started the healing inside of me, just by being herself. And when I left, I made the biggest mistake in my life. I left her behind."

"You left us behind," Melora reminded him.

"Yeah…" He nodded. "I guess I did." He looked away briefly then turned back to ask, "I need to know something. Was she okay after I left? What kind of mother was she to you?"

"She was the best mom I could have," Melora answered quietly. "She sang to me when I couldn't sleep. She hugged me every morning and kissed me goodnight every time I closed my eyes at the end of the day. We didn't have very much but I knew I was loved and that made me special. When she died my whole world was gone."

"What happened?" Mountain asked. His hand tightened on his coffee cup.

"She was crossing the street to go to her second job when a car ran her down. The guy behind the wheel was drunk and he tried to get away but his car was damaged. He hit her so hard she flew about twenty feet and he crashed into a mailbox. He got out and just started screaming at her. She was lying there on the road bleeding and he told her she wrecked his car. He was more worried about the damage to his car than he was for her. Someone on the sidewalk called 911. When the cops got there, he was still screaming about his insurance. She died on the way to the hospital." Melora dried the tears on her face but she didn't look at him.

"What happened to him?"

She shrugged. "I was a kid, so nobody ever told me. But I found out years later. The bastard went to court and claimed Mom ran out in front of him and he couldn't stop. Officer Daniels told the courts his blood alcohol was twice the legal limit and the judge sentenced him to a year on probation. Told the man he couldn't drink anymore."

Mountain scoffed. "I don't believe that."

"Yeah, he didn't either. The next week he was stopped and they found him drunk again. He spent the next three weeks in jail."

"Did it help?"

She shook her head. "Not a bit. Within a week after getting out, he was in a crash that killed three people. The judge sent him to prison for two years."

"Did he learn anything from his time in the slammer?"

"No he didn't." She met her father's eyes. "But he learned it a week later." She lifted her cup to her lips and didn't say anything else.

Mountain didn't ask either.

Before their conversation could continue, Sam came out of the room. He paused for a moment then made his way to their table. Grabbing a cup, he poured them all a fresh cup of coffee. "So do you have any idea what Raven will do when he gets here?" he asked as he gazed at Mountain.

Mountain stared at the other man with a hard look. "Raven is a good man and he runs a tight club. That Whiskey did what he did isn't going to sit well with him. Whiskey's been in trouble before and this time, he went over the line."

"Have you heard anything about this in the last two years?" Melora spoke up.

"Actually, I have." Mountain nodded. "I was in Raleigh last year making a run to Raven's club and the cops thought they found a piece of Baily's shirt. The cops came over to the club and talked to Raven. They said someone was hiking in the woods and found a place where the hogs were digging. They found three pieces of cloth that didn't belong there. Raven was crazy, wondering what the hell happened. Now, I guess we know."

"Was there anyone in his club who tried to play it down?" Melora asked. She still had one secret but she wasn't willing to share it just yet.

"There was one man and his woman. I think his name was Jonesy. He said the cloth could have been anyone's. He didn't think it proved anything. He tried awful hard to get everyone to think Baily just took off."

"I can't believe Jonesy ever had a woman." Melora scoffed. "He doesn't usually go that way."

Mountain chuckled. "Yeah, well Izzy didn't seem to appreciate him either."

Melora sat up straight and turned her head to Mountain. "Izzy?"

"Yeah. Little bit of a thing, long dark red hair and—"

"Green eyes?" Melora looked pissed. "That son of a bitch, that dirty rotten son of a bitch."

"Who?" Sam asked.

"Whiskey." Melora seethed. "Whiskey has control of Izzy. Every fucking time I called her, she told him where I was. Now I know why he was right behind me every time I changed cities."

"How do you know she just didn't give you up?" Mountain asked.

"Because Izzy wouldn't have done that, not to me," Melora defended. "Jonesy isn't a good man, if she's with him it wouldn't be because she cared for him. He's a pervert that likes little boys. Izzy is too smart for that."

"How do you know?" Sam asked.

"Izzy and I met when we were both sixteen. I'd just ran away from yet another foster home and she had walked away from hell she lived with. We hooked up from necessity but became friends that winter. When you have no warm place to live and there's no food, you tend to appreciate who you're sharing a place with. We had to steal to live that winter and I taught her how to do it without getting busted. We also learned self-defense together. I had her back and she had mine. Now those bastards are using her to get to me."

"How do you figure that?" Sam asked.

"We made a vow eight years ago. We vowed no matter what happened in our lives we would always have each other's backs. If she's with Jonesy right now, she doesn't have a choice. Whiskey threatened to kill her and she probably thinks her best bet and mine is to give them the information they need and..." Melora stopped and thought about something. She snapped her fingers. "Of course, that's what she's doing."

"What are you talking about?" Mountain asked.

"She's been trying to tell me all this time." Melora looked distracted as she thought about it. "I didn't put it together until right now."

"I think you need to explain," Sam urged.

"Every time I called her to let her know I was okay and where I was, she reminded me I wasn't alone. As long as I had her, I would never be alone and that she had my back. I thought she was giving me encouragement but she wasn't, she was trying to tell me they were watching her."

"What are you going to do?" Mountain asked.

"I'm going to get her out of there," Melora vowed.

"How the hell are you gonna do that when you're here and she's there?" Deke asked as he joined them.

"I don't know but I need to get her out of harm's way," Melora replied in a firm tone.

"Maybe I can help with that," a voice rumbled from the front door.

Everyone turned to see an older man standing there. His hair was long and black. His face looked worn and there was a scruff of black along his jaw. His eyes were dark and at the moment there was a stormy expression in them. He was dressed in a black t-shirt and jeans. The only color on him was on the leather vest he wore. He stood there with nine other men and all of them looked tired and ornery.

"Raven, welcome," Deke stated.

Gator, Sam and Mountain all got to their feet.

Melora just stared at the man.

Chapter Seven

Raven made his way to their table. He hadn't taken his eyes off Melora. He reached for the coffee pot and poured some coffee into a cup. When he brought it to his lips, he finally looked away from her. After he took a gulp of the hot brew, he reached out his hand to Deke.

After Deke, he shook Gator's hand then Sam's. "Good to see you again my old friend." He turned to Reva and asked for more coffee.

Raven's men stepped forward and each of them grabbed a cup.

Raven turned to Mountain. "Good to see you too, old man."

"Well, it is and again it isn't," Mountain agreed as they shook hands.

Deke observed the men Raven brought with him. Turning to the other leader he asked, "Who are your men? I think you should know we're on lockdown and having this many strangers is making me a bit jumpy."

Raven glanced at his men and nodded. "I don't blame you. This is Gunny, Rembrandt, Conner, Sal, Gremlin, Big Tony, Trainer, Fubar, and Grandy." He paused then glared at Deke. "You understand why I had to bring a small army. A threat has been made against me and the Ghosts and I need to learn the truth behind it, then I need to act on that truth to resolve it. I didn't want to bring this to your town but I have no choice."

Deke nodded. "I do understand and I want to help. I don't want this feud any more than you do and I hope we can keep the casualties down to a minimum."

"Yeah, well I understand that I've been lied to for the last two years. I want to know how and why," Raven commented. He turned to Melora and said, "I hear you're in some trouble with one of my men."

Melora snorted. "Whiskey isn't much of a man, more like a parasite, a blood sucking mealy mouth worm."

"Yeah, he's been off the grid for a while now," Raven agreed. "Been thinking about cutting him loose then I heard he was trailing a woman who might have murdered Baily Walker. Senator Walker wants you really bad. He wants to know what happened to the kid."

"So Whiskey blamed this on me?" She sneered. "That figures. He always was a pig." She got to her feet and reached into her back pocket. Deke had returned her phone to her earlier. She searched through her phone and brought up the video then handed it to Raven. "This is what really happened that night."

As Raven watched the video, his frown deepened. His face turned to stone when it finished. He handed the phone back to Melora. Turning to Deke, he shook his head. "Whiskey's a dead man, he just doesn't know it yet."

"He's got at least two other men with him and there's another man at your club," Deke informed him. "Melora thinks the woman Izzy is being held hostage against her will in order to give them information on where Melora is."

"Yeah, that sounds about right." Raven nodded. "Izzy has proven she doesn't want to be with him but until she says something no one else will help her." He shrugged. "That's just the way it is in our club."

"She won't say anything until she has no other choice," Melora added. "You need to get her away from Jonesy and keep her safe until Whiskey is caught."

Raven nodded. "Don't worry about Jonesy. He's earned his pain. The club will take care of him."

"I don't care about Jonesy, Micah or Lightning. They had their chance to stop him but they didn't. They even helped him get rid of Baily's body and helped to cover up his death and disappearance. As far as I'm concerned, they can fry alongside Whiskey." Melora seethed.

"The only problem is how are we gonna stop Whiskey?" Sam asked.

"We lure him into thinking he's gonna get to me," Melora answered.

"That's not going to happen," Mountain assured her. "He isn't going to even breathe the same air as you if I have anything to say about it."

"That makes two of us." Sam growled.

"It's the only way to draw him out," Melora protested. "We know he's close but we don't know where exactly. I thought I heard his bike in town a couple days ago but I haven't seen him yet. Nor have I called Izzy either. He might be waiting and searching Boston for me yet. She told him I was there over a week ago. All we do is let him close enough, then you guys can take him. I don't care what happens to him once you guys get a hold of him. Micah and Lightning either. They've been chasing me for two fucking years and I'm tired of jumping at shadows and living in the cold. This needs to be over."

"If I'm not mistaken Iceman saw Whiskey and his group here yesterday," Deke spoke up. "I can't say anyone has seen him since then though."

"Why didn't you send me the video two years ago?" Raven asked. "If you had, you wouldn't have had to run at all."

Melora glared at him. "I don't know you man. How was I supposed to know you would stand up for me against one of your own?"

"You could have asked anyone here." Raven shrugged.

"I didn't know anyone here two days ago, let alone two years ago." She scoffed. "Besides, I wouldn't have trusted them anymore than I would have trusted you at that point."

"And why is that?" Raven wanted to know.

Melora sneered as she flicked her fingers toward his cut but she knew better than to touch it. When she was younger, one of the waitresses at the bar she worked at had done just that, touched a member's cut, as they call it, and she'd been hurt for it. They broke her fingers. Bikers didn't want you to touch them unless they meant something to you. "People fear this vest for a reason. I didn't know I could trust it, not then. I would watch your men and let's just say, I wasn't impressed by their actions."

"You feared what you did not know." Raven shrugged. "That's hardly my fault."

"True enough, but I was smart enough to steer clear. I've seen bikers hurt the people I worked with before, just for touching their cuts. I've had enough heartbreak in my life. I was barely surviving and it hasn't gotten any better since then." She shook her head. "Whiskey isn't holding together very well. The last time I saw him, he looked like he was coming down off a bad high. He was dirty, jittery and had a bad case of the munchies. Micah and Lightning didn't look so good either. They looked disgusted with him."

Raven shook his head. "I haven't seen Whiskey in two months. When I did see him, he told me he had a tip on you and was following through. He vowed to bring you back in one piece, so I could question you about Baily's disappearance."

"Now you know that was nothing more than a lie," Melora grumbled. "One piece, my ass."

Raven stared at her for a moment. "Have you actually seen him here yet?"

"Not seen him no, but I've heard his bike."

Raven frowned. "You've heard his bike? What the hell does that mean? One ride sounds the same as any other."

Melora shook her head. "No it doesn't. His bike has a particular whine. It's the stuff nightmares are made of."

Raven snorted out loud. "Now, I know you're making this shit up."

Melora shrugged. "Not really. Each bike has a different sound to it. Maybe you don't notice it but I do. His bike has chased me for two years, if you don't think I know the sound of it, then you're the crazy one."

"One thing you should know, Raven," Mountain interjected while looking concerned about Melora's attitude toward Raven. "Melora is my kid and that bastard isn't getting close to her."

Raven raised his eyebrow. "Your kid? I didn't think you had any kids."

"I only found out about her four years ago. I never thought I'd find her but I did. I'm not going to lose her again, not to some psycho. Especially...not to Whiskey." He glanced over at Sam but didn't say anything. That would be another discussion for another time.

Sam just glared back at Mountain.

Melora looked from her father to her lover and growled. "Both of you need to put your cocks back in your pants and behave. I don't have time for either of you right now."

Raven frowned as he looked from Mountain to Sam. "Is there something going on here that I should know about?"

"Not that it's any of your business, or anyone else's but..." Melora nodded. "I'm sleeping with this one..." She pointed at Sam. "...And my 'father' doesn't like it." She air quoted the word *father*.

Raven paused then nodded. "I can see why. Sam is older than he is."

She shrugged. "It's my choice and Mountain doesn't get a say in my life unless I say so. For all my life, he's been nothing more than a donor and if he wants to be more he has to prove himself." She shrugged. "Right now, we have other things to worry about." She got to her feet. "You need to prove something right here, right now." She pointed her finger into Raven's chest.

"What might that be?" Raven asked, though his dark eyes narrowed. Curious to know just how far she was willing to push him. Not many people demanded from him and he liked it that way.

"You need to get Izzy out from Jonesy's control." Melora began to pace. "I need to know she's safe before we get to Whiskey."

"Okay," Raven replied. "I'll give you that but lady... you need to be very careful what you demand from me. I don't usually do orders from anyone. You and I aren't fucking and you ain't my mother or my sister, so you can't make demands from me."

Melora sneered but didn't say anything.

"I'll put a call into my VP. Silas will make sure Izzy gets free of Jonesy and that he's held until we get back for questioning." Raven reached for his phone and placed the call. A few minutes later, he gave her a nod. Turning to study the rest of the group, he asked, "So how do you want this to go down?"

"I told you, let me lure him into thinking he can get to me, then before he does you guys get to him," Melora explained.

"And we said *that* wasn't going to happen," Mountain stated firmly.

Melora turned to him and practically hissed. "If he sees or hears that Raven and his guys are here, he'll run, he'll go so far underground we'll never find him, and we'll lose him. Then I'll be looking over my shoulder for the rest of my life and I'm not doing that anymore. I need this pig caught and taken care of. I can't live in fear another day." She paused, then looked around at all the bikers. "I'm doing this with or without you guys, so either get on board or get the hell out of my way."

"And how exactly are you planning on luring him in?" Raven asked with sarcasm.

Melora smiled but the humor never reached her eyes. She reached for her phone and dialed a number. When they heard someone answer, she put the phone on speaker and spoke, "Hey Whiskey, my name is Melora, and I think you've been looking for me. I just heard a rumor about you and I have to ask, is it true you are nothing more than a liar and a cheat? You killed a man and told everyone that I did it. You've been chasing me for two years now and I'm tired of playing you're fucked up games. You want me, come get me, bastard!"

"Where are you bitch?" they heard him swear with a growl in his voice.

"You can find me in Troy, New York. I'll be the one standing alongside the road giving you the finger. I hope you showered since I last saw you in Boston. You were looking a bit ripe that day. I could smell your stench from twenty feet away. Your hands were shaking so bad, you couldn't even hold that big old bloody knife you used to slice Baily up with."

"How did you know about that?" he asked.

"I got it all on video, asshat." She sneered. "Maybe Senator Walker would like to see it. At least then, he could blame the right person for what happened."

"He'd never believe it. I'll tell him the video was doctored and he'll be stupid enough to believe me," Whiskey assured her. "I've been working on him and telling him Raven can't get the job done but I could."

Melora caught Raven's eyes. "You been bad mouthing your club president? Wow, that's like slapping him in the face. You're either a very brave man or very stupid. Me, I'm voting for you, being just plain stupid."

"Yeah and when I take your body back to Walker I'll have the political power to take the club from Raven. I'll have the power Raven wants but doesn't have."

"You think Raven will give up his patch that easy?"

"He won't have a choice," Whiskey foolishly told her. "And when that club is mine, I'll take it places Raven never would. We'll be running dope and guns up and down the East coast and there won't be anyone to stop us."

"You still have to find me first," she taunted.

"Don't worry about that. I'll find you and drag your carcass back to North Carolina. But first, I think I'll fuck you for a while. I'd been watching you for a while before that night. You never know you might like it and it might keep you alive for a day or two longer. Then I'll take you out where we left Baily and you can share the same fate he did. No one will ever know what happened to you, just like Baily."

Melora laughed. "Too bad, Baily didn't stay there. The hogs never got him." Then she hung up the call. She glanced over at Sam and then to her father. Finally looking at Raven, she shrugged. "The boy's got ambition, I'll give him that. Maybe not dealing with reality but he's got dreams. He don't seem to like you at all."

"I'm gonna grind his bones into dust." Raven swore through gritted teeth. "I'm gonna start at his feet and work my way up and he'll still be alive when I do it. I'm gonna enjoy hearing him beg for his life." Running his fingers through his hair he glared at her. "What did you mean when you told him the hogs didn't get Baily?"

Melora shivered at Raven's descriptions of revenge. She almost felt sorry for Whiskey...almost. Even if he didn't actually do what he said, she knew Raven was not someone to piss off and right now he was pissed at Whiskey. "I hope you make it hurt, he deserves nothing less." She shrugged, then added, "Someone may have moved the body before the hogs got the scent of his blood."

"What happened to his body?" Mountain asked.

"It's safe that's all I'm going to say."

Deke got up and went to join Zipper in his corner. After speaking to him for a minute, he came back to the table. "I have Zipper tracing Melora's last call. He should be able to tell us where Whiskey is."

"That might help," Raven replied. "But how are we going to lure him to us?"

"Before we do that, I think Senator Walker needs to know what happened the night Baily disappeared," Melora suggested. "Whiskey's been lying to him and blaming me for what happened. I didn't even think about Walker coming after me too. At least if we show him what happened, he'll know the truth."

Mountain nodded. "That's a good idea baby."

Melora snapped her head in his direction. "I'm not your *baby*. I'm a woman full grown."

Mountain's lips thinned and his eyes narrowed at the tone of her voice. "You're my daughter whether you like it or not. Neither of us can change that no matter what we really feel."

Melora's lips thinned and her eyes narrowed as she glared at the man who was her father. "You can't just barge into my life at this point and start telling me what to do. I've been making decisions about what I want to do and what I want in my life for years now. I have kept myself alive without the help of a man too. I understand you didn't know about me until recently, but you know what? I did know about you." She kept glaring at him as she continued, "I listened to my mother talk about a man she met years before and maybe in my mind, I knew some of what she told me was a fantasy on her part but I don't know what kind of man you've become. So please don't tell me what to do or think. I can do that for myself. My mother taught me how and I've learned the rest of it on my own."

"Did you ever think for one moment that I would like the chance to know you?" Mountain asked.

Melora leaned over the table toward him. "Then get to know the woman in front of you, not the little girl I was a long time ago. That little girl is all grown up now. I can't go back to being her again."

"Are you even gonna give me a chance?" Mountain asked. "Or will you let the bitterness of me not being in your life hold you back?"

Melora sat back and stared at him for a moment then nodded. "That's what I've been doing huh? Ok, I see your point. All I can say is I will try, if you can, I can too." She got to her feet. "But first we have a killer to find."

"I think you should send the video to Walker first thing," Raven interjected. "He's got a bounty out on your head and he needs to rescind it. Or at least, get it on the right person's head. Whiskey thinks he's got clout with Walker behind him. Let's take that clout away, then we can hunt him down."

Zipper got up and disappeared for a moment, when he returned he had a vest with him. Handing it to Melora, he explained, "This vest has a tracking unit in it. Wear it at all times. If he does manage to get to you, at least we'll know where to find you."

Melora slipped the vest on. It claimed she belonged to the Sin's Bastards.

When Mountain saw it, he growled but didn't say anything.

Sam grinned but didn't say anything either.

"First, let's give Senator Walker something to think about." Melora pulled out her phone and wrote a quick email to the Senator from the number Raven gave her. She told him who she was and what the video was all about, then she told him what Whiskey's future plans were. She told him he could view the video anytime he wanted to find out the truth, then told him where she was, she hit the send button and closed her phone. Slipping the phone back into her pocket Melora casually poured herself another cup of coffee. Before she could take a sip, her phone rang.

When she answered the call, she heard Izzy on the other end. "Hey girl!"

"Are you okay?"

"I am now." She chuckled. "Thank you for getting me free of this creep, although it took you long enough."

"I'm so sorry. I didn't put it together until now," Melora replied quietly. "I guess I didn't listen very well did I?"

"No, but you listened when it counted and that's all that matters," Izzy reminded her. "You got me out of there. Jonesy had just gotten a call from Whiskey and he wasn't happy about it."

"What did they do to you?"

"That's a story for another day," Izzy said. "Can I come where you are? I really need to see for myself that you're still alive."

"Yeah, I'm in Troy, New York. Staying with some friends."

"Okay baby girl, I'm on my way." Izzy laughed.

"Yeah, yeah. It ought to be interesting anyway. I'm staying with the Sin's Bastards MC, I found my father and he's one of the Sons of Satan MC and Raven from the Ghosts of Dixie is here and everyone is hunting Whiskey."

"Wow, you guys are going after Whiskey?" Izzy's voice held fear. "You be careful girl, he wants you dead. Hopefully before anyone knows the truth."

"Yeah, the man is crazy. He put the blame for Baily on my head. But it's too late, people know the truth now, Raven, Walker and everyone here knows what really happened. At least I don't have to run anymore. And I got one more card to play that he don't know about."

"What did you do? What are you talking about, one more card?"

"Hey, we'll talk about that when you get here. I want to see for myself that you're all right."

"I'll be there sometime tomorrow. Love you baby girl. Please be careful. Whiskey is a mean sonofabitch."

"Love you too. I'll be careful. He isn't gonna get me, not now." Melora hung up the call and turned back to the table. Everyone was staring at her. "What?"

"What are you planning?" Mountain asked. "You said you had one more card to play?"

"Yeah, what might that be?" Raven asked.

Melora frowned. "If I told you it wouldn't be a surprise now would it?"

"I think you'd better tell us anyway," Deke demanded. "I, for one, don't like surprises."

"I plan to turn the tables on Whiskey. He thinks he's got me just where he wants me, on the run and afraid of him. Well, I'm tired of living in fear. Now it's his turn to be afraid. All I ever needed was for one person to believe in me, just one." She turned to look at Sam. "And now I have that."

Sam gazed steadily back at her.

"So what are you going to do?" Raven asked.

"I need to find a way to get the underground looking for him. Every city has them and they're the people you see every day and tend to overlook. He thinks he's free and clear to move around the city looking for me. But I know him better than he knows himself. Right now, he's so strung out on dope he doesn't know shit. If we play on his fears and paranoia, we can send him over the edge. We need to split Micah and Lightning away from him. There's one thing I've noticed about Whiskey, he doesn't do so well by himself. He has to have somebody to order around. Alone, he's a damn coward, that's why he always has someone with him."

"What underground are you going to get to look for him?" Deke asked.

"How about the guys at Redemption House?" Cassie asked from behind them. She and Peaches had joined the group a while ago but hadn't wanted to get involved in the conversation.

"Who and what is Redemption House?" Raven asked.

Melora smiled. "That would be perfect. Do you know them well enough to ask?"

"Redemption House is my dream," Cassie replied. "I know it well and I know the guys would be happy to help."

Sam nodded. "Your idea might just work."

"What is Redemption House?" Raven repeated his question.

"It's a half-way house for people that need a second chance. The guys who work there are homeless vets. They lived on the streets and know everyone," Cassie explained. "If anyone can do this, they can. They can be your underground team. In fact, I'll bet they would think this great fun."

"This isn't supposed to be fun, Spitfire." Deke growled. "This guy is crazy and could hurt somebody."

Cassie walked over to her husband and cupped his face between her hands. "Honey, these men know what they're doing. They've been to places you and I will never even know about. They have put their lives on the line for their country and been spit and stomped on for their efforts. They can do this, all we have to do is ask. I'm willing to ask."

"I've been to Redemption House and I watched these men," Melora interjected. "I've even spoken to some of them. When you've lived on the streets you know how to hide, how to watch what's going on around you and how to disappear when you need to. In fact, it was one of those men who told me about the warehouse behind the shop. He said it would be warm and dry and safe."

Cassie smiled. "Frankie or Gus?"

"Gus."

Cassie looked around at everyone assembled. "These men know this city, every nook and cranny. They know every side street and every dead end. They can watch this city and no one will ever know they are even there.

Melora grinned. "It was Frankie in fact, who gave me the idea. He was talking about how they play this game. They follow someone they don't know just to find out what they do. It doesn't hurt anyone and he claims it keeps their skills sharp." She turned to Gator. "They followed you one day just for shits and giggles."

Gator held up his hands. "I don't want to know and neither does anyone else."

"Are you sure about that?" She teased. "They were impressed."

"Drop it, woman." He growled.

"Okay, okay, your secrets are safe with me," Melora assured him. "If we're going to do this, we have to get these guys in place before Whiskey gets here."

"He's about an hour out, boss," Zipper announced. Looking up from his computer he told them, "He was coming from the Boston area. Not the city itself but the same area."

Deke stared at the others then looked over at Cassie. "Can you get them moving? Set up a perimeter and tell them to watch for anyone wearing a Ghosts vest. They all three should be together at this point. Tell them to just watch but not to engage. We just want eyes on them."

"Yeah, I can do that." Cassie nodded.

"Please tell them thank you from me." Melora looked at Cassie. "They don't really know me but I appreciate their help."

Cassie paused and stared at her, like she knew just about all there was to Melora...She had lived a life similar to hers. Then she nodded.

Chapter Eight

A little more than an hour later, Cassie answered her phone. When she hung up, she grinned. "That was Amos. He's out on highway 90 and just saw three riders come into town wearing Ghost colors."

"Okay, it should take them some time to find a place to stay and get settled," Raven concluded.

Melora smiled. "Let's shake things up a bit."

"What are you going to do?" Mountain asked with a frown.

"Desperate men make mistakes and we need Whiskey to start making mistakes." She reached for her phone and called him. "Hey Whiskey, are you here yet? I'm getting bored waiting for you."

"Fuck you bitch!" Whiskey growled. "Where the hell are you?"

"I'm in the shadows all around you. I'll see you but you'll never see me," Melora taunted him and hung up.

"It's dangerous to push a man like that," Raven warned.

Melora shrugged. "I want him to come unhinged. I want him paranoid, scared of his own shadow. He's made me crazy the last two years."

"You might just piss him off," Sam added his warning.

"I want him to feel at least a small bit of the fear I've felt these last two years," Melora admitted.

"Be careful what you wish for girl, it might be more than you can handle," Mountain muttered.

Melora stared out the window. She didn't see the front yard, instead she saw the many towns and places she'd been in over the last two years. From Raleigh, to Charlotte, Newport News to Dover, Trenton, to Boston and finally to Troy. She thought she would be safe in the bigger cities but that hadn't been the case. He found her nearly everywhere she went. She'd been cold and wet while living in fear every day for over eight hundred days. She'd given him that kind of power over her and now she was taking it back. "Okay, I'll back off but I'm not giving up. As long as he's under surveillance, I can let him alone for now."

"Let the guys watch him for a while," Cassie suggested. "They'll keep him under surveillance. He won't be able to move without someone seeing him."

Melora shook her head. "I don't want anyone getting in his way, or getting hurt. He'd go through anyone standing in his way."

"Honey, these men are vets," Cassie explained. "They know how to watch someone without getting caught. He won't even know they're there."

Sam got up and went over to her. Wrapping his arms around her, he pulled her close and Melora let him. He simply held her.

Deke noticed Mountain didn't like the fact his dad was so close. He didn't say anything but his lips tightened and he glared at Sam.

"As long as Whiskey is under watch, does anyone mind if I take a nap?" Raven asked. "That was one long ass trip."

Deke got to his feet. "Sure, I'll show you where you can bunk. We're on lockdown so my men have the place guarded."

Raven and his men followed Deke down the hall.

~* * * *~

Mountain sat there glaring at Sam.

Melora finally went to the kitchen to get something to eat.

Sam went back over to the table and sat down. The silence between them was stifled and heavy. Finally, Sam lifted his head and glared at Mountain. "Look man, I know you want to punch me right now, but can we get past it? We have a woman to protect and she means something different to both of us."

"Do you love her?" Mountain asked.

Sam shrugged. "How the hell would I know that? We only met the other day."

"And yet you slept with her already?" Mountain sneered.

Sam shook his head. "You don't know anything about how we met or what happened after that, so don't judge me or her. You don't have that right."

"Let's both agree to disagree until this Whiskey character is taken out of the equation." Mountain shrugged. "Then you and me are going to dance but not until my girl is safe."

They both turned when they heard laughter coming from the kitchen. Melora stood there with little Sammy in her arms while Cassie held Jemmia in hers. Both women were laughing at the antics of the children.

"Who is she holding?" Mountain asked. "She looks good with a baby in her arms."

Sam grinned. "That's my grandson Sam. Cassie has his sister."

"Twins?" the other man asked. "That's cool. How old are they?"

"About six months or so." Sam shrugged. "They are a bit small because Cassie had them early, but they're growing like weeds."

"Babies have a way of doing that," Mountain agreed.

"So what's the story with you and Melora?" Sam asked. "Why weren't you there when she was born?"

Mountain shrugged. "I'd just gotten out of the service a few months before I met her mother. Bought a bike and took off looking to find myself. Met Carla in Chicago. Left after about a week and never looked back. Found my place in Texas. Guess I shouldn't have left but I was still hurting and I needed to find a purpose. Then with the MC there wasn't a place for her in my life at the time. Wouldn't have been good for her."

Sam nodded. "Been there done that. I never knew I had a kid either until he was twelve. Brought him home with me and made a mess of things for the next six years. He got the hell out as soon as he could. Came looking for him about eight months ago and almost messed it all up again. I got a second chance and I'm hoping you do too." He paused and leaned forward, "But know something here. Whether we stay together or not, isn't up to you. It's up to me and her."

"And you think she'll chose you once this is all over?"

"Maybe, maybe not? Who knows?" Sam shrugged. "I'm hoping that we can come to an agreement, so she doesn't have to make a choice. If that happens we all lose."

"And you would just let her walk away?"

"If that's what she really wants." Sam again, shrugged. "I don't have to force women to stay with me."

"I just want a chance to know my daughter," Mountain stated quietly. "This situation is just wrong. I finally find her and there is a possibility I could lose her to a psycho like fucken Whiskey? I can't lose her." He ran his fingers through his hair. "I never thought I'd get this chance before. I mean me having a kid? I was always careful not to let that happen. I didn't know I could take care of a kid, then four years ago this dude contacts me, telling me I not only had a kid but she was already full grown. But as soon as he told me, I thought of Carla. She was the only woman who would've had my child. She was the only woman who loved me longer than the moment we were together. I never should have left her like I did."

"Hindsight is wonderful ain't it?" Sam chuckled. "Had a bit of it myself a few years back."

Mountain searched and found his daughter in the kitchen. His eyes softened when he looked at her. "Wish I could have watched her grow up. I missed out on all of that."

"So find a woman and have another child." Sam shrugged.

"It wouldn't be the same."

"Fate is sometimes a cruel bitch."

Deke joined them and shortly after he did, Cassie came out from the kitchen. "Gus just called. Whiskey and two of his men just found an abandoned warehouse over by the shop. They seem to be settling in for the moment."

"At least we know where they are," Deke commented as he took his daughter from his wife. He glanced over at Mountain. "Tell us what you know about this guy they call Whiskey. Have you met him before?"

Mountain nodded. "Yeah, I've met him. Never really cared for him though. When I first started doing business with Raven's club, ten years ago, he was one of those guys that sat at the back of the room and watched everyone else. The last few years, he's been working his way up. He likes the limelight and pushing other guys around. Likes to make himself out to be more important than he really is. He always had at least two or three men around him." Mountain shook his head. "When we heard earlier that he had plans to take over the club from Raven I wasn't really surprised. He's plain crazy if he thinks he can do it. The men under Raven won't allow that to happen. And his idea for running guns and dope on the East coast is just his own dream. Even with Walker in his pocket, he'd never be able to do it. That's just plain dumb."

"Not to mention very illegal." Sam snorted. "How the hell did he think he was gonna do that? Walker would never allow it. His political career means everything to him. He wouldn't risk it for that."

"How do you know Walker?" Deke asked his dad.

Sam snorted. "Everyone knows Walker. He's big in the political world and lately, he's been sprouting some nonsense about turning back the illegals from his state. Says if they want to come here they should do it legally, instead of just walking across the border."

"Well, he's right about that," Mountain agreed. "But that's not what we should be worried about right now."

"Now that he knows what really happened, Whiskey should be the one who's worried," Deke noted.

Mountain shook his head. "I don't think it'll make a difference. Whiskey is to the point where he thinks he's untouchable."

"No one is untouchable," Melora told her father. "What Whiskey doesn't know is that I know where Baily's body is."

"How is that possible?" Sam asked.

She shrugged. "Before I left town I collected his body and took it to a safe place. When this is over, I'll tell Senator Walker where it is. He can see for himself what really happened."

"Won't the evidence be destroyed by now?" Mountain asked.

Melora shook her head. "I made sure it was preserved well enough. He'll be able to see for himself what happened."

"Does anyone else know about this?" Mountain frowned.

"No, I made sure of that," Melora replied with confidence. "A secret is only kept when one person knows it. My momma didn't raise no fool."

Mountain chuckled. "She sure didn't."

Deke got to his feet and handed Jemmia back to Cassie. "And on that note, I'm going to tell the men outside to be alert. Now that Whiskey is here, everyone needs to be more on watch. I don't want him anywhere near my family."

Melora sat down and reached for the coffee. Something finally caught her eye and as she looked up, she gasped. She found herself staring at the painting of a white tiger on the wall. All she could do was stare at the animal. "What the hell?" she whispered. "How did I miss that?"

Sam chuckled when he noticed her gaze. "Well, things have been a little crazy since you got here."

Mountain turned to see what she was looking at. "Wow, he's beautiful. Who painted him?"

"I did," Cassie admitted. "When the three clubs came together, they needed a new mascot."

"Three clubs?" Mountain frowned.

"Deke was President of the Satan's Spawn when Iceman came over," Sam explained. "He was President of the Sinner's from Boston and I was President of Satan's Bastards from Maine...Anyway, when we all decided to stay here, Deke combined our clubs into his own, and we all became Sin's Bastards."

"When did all this take place?" Mountain asked.

"Not too long ago, maybe six months or so."

"What's his name?" Melora whispered, not having taken her eyes off the painting.

"His name is Cade but don't tell anyone." Cassie leaned in to whisper in her ear, "I'm not sure the guys would appreciate my giving him a name. He became the symbol of the new club."

Melora shivered as she stared at the tiger from a dream she had at fourteen. She couldn't believe she'd finally found him. For so long, he'd been a figment of her imagination but seeing him like this made him so very real. She turned her head to Cassie and for a moment, neither said anything.

Then Cassie whispered, "You've met him before haven't you?"

Melora nodded. "In a dream a long time ago."

"So he means something to you?" Cassie turned around and stared at the painting of Rufus and Diablo. "They mean something to me too."

Melora turned to see the paintings. "Did you feel like they kept you safe when you were a child?"

Cassie turned and gazed intently at Melora. "How did you know?"

Melora turned and stared at the white tiger. "Cuz he did the same thing for me. I kept him in a safe place in my mind but he was there when I needed him the most. He was always there."

Cassie wrapped her arms around the other woman. "We have more in common than we realized. Know always that you are welcome here and I will keep you safe."

Melora patted Cassie's arms. "No you can't promise that but as long as I have him, I'll be okay." She turned to her. "But how did you know? You painted him exactly the way I saw him in my dream, right down to the chipped tooth on the right side of his mouth."

"When the guys asked me to do the painting I just saw him in my mind." Cassie shook her head. "I can't explain it any other way than that. I just saw him in my mind."

Melora felt tears running down her face.

When Sam noticed this, he joined the women and wrapped his arms around Melora. "What's going on?"

Melora turned in his arms and burst into tears. Sobbing, she just held him for a moment.

Sam looked over the top of her head at Cassie.

Cassie motioned to the painting, then at Melora. "He means something to her."

Sam frowned. "What could a painting mean to her?"

Cassie smiled softly. "He's her protector."

"I don't understand." Sam shook his head.

"You don't have to." Cassie shook her head. "She does and that's what matters."

Sam nudged Melora's head up. When she looked at him he asked, "Are you okay?"

Melora nodded. "I will be now that he's here." She turned and looked at the painting again. "I never thought I'd find him."

Sam was going to say something but he saw Cassie shake her head. Instead, he listened.

Mountain got up and joined them.

"When I was a kid, after I lost my mom I went into foster care," Melora whispered. "I hated never belonging anywhere, living in someone else's house, sleeping in someone else's bed. I was always alone and I hated it. I missed my mom so much. Then one night, I cried myself to sleep again, only this time it was different. I started dreaming. I dreamt of my mother. I was remembering all the good times we had together." She shrugged. "I know we didn't have much, all the other kids made sure they told me that. They used to rub it in that they always had more than I did but it didn't matter. We had each other and I had something they didn't. I had a mom who loved me beyond reason. Anyway, that night in my dream, my mom said she had a reason for visiting me. She told me that I had a protector and he would always be there for me when I was feeling lonely or scared. She said he would keep the ghosties away from my soul and as long as I believed in her, he would be with me."

Sam looked troubled as Melora's hands tightened on his arms.

"Mom told me she couldn't always be there and that someday, I wouldn't need her there anymore, but I would always have him." Melora's words were little more than a whisper at this point. "I told her I would always need her and I would never let her out of my heart and she smiled. She told me I would always have her but I would always have the tiger too."

"Did she ever tell you his name?" Cassie whispered.

Melora smiled. "She called him Cade too."

Cassie's eyes widened. "Oh, my Gosh..."

"What else did she tell you?" Mountain asked.

"She told me he would keep me safe," Melora replied as she turned in Sam's arms to look at him. "Maybe that's why I feel safe here in this place, in your arms....That's why I feel connected to you."

Sam grinned. "I'll never let you go now. I think I'll keep you."

Mountain growled deep in his throat.

Melora turned to her father. "Behave yourself."

Mountain gave her a disgusted look.

Cassie tried to hide her smile as she watched the three of them.

"Right now, I want to bathe in the awesomeness that I finally found him." Melora nodded. "I never thought he was real until now. He was always my little secret before. Something I had but no one else knew about." She sighed. "I don't know what the future will be but I do know that for now I'm safe as long as I stay near him, I'll be okay. I never realized how much he helped me to get through the difficult times until now. He was there for me when I thought I had no one." She chuckled. "Oh course, Izzy never understood it but that's ok, she didn't have to."

"Tell us about Izzy again?" Mountain asked. His expression showed that he didn't appreciate the fact Sam's arms were around his daughter, nor the fact that she didn't seem to mind.

Melora sighed. "Izzy and I met when we were sixteen as I told you before. I had just run away from yet another foster home where I didn't mean shit to anybody. No one there cared whether I was there or not, so I decided not to be. She had run away from home. Her father liked to drink and her mom was just worn out. They both shut her out and she couldn't stay there anymore. I guess I didn't blame her. Separately, we each had our own problems but together, we had each other and we never forgot that. We stayed together after that. We had each other's back and together, we survived in Chicago for two years. We lived on the streets, just under the gaze of society. We did everything together and we got as close as sisters. And when we left Chicago for other places, we went together. When we hit Raleigh, she stayed when I left. I couldn't take her with me. I wouldn't put her life on the line either. I hated that I left her behind, especially now that I know Whiskey got to her but she'll be here soon and we can be together again."

Cassie smiled. "I have a friend like that."

"Are you sure you want to be with her again?" Mountain scoffed. "She did give you up."

Melora shook her head. "She didn't betray me. She didn't have any other choice but to do what she did."

"She still told him where you were."

Melora shook her head again. "She might have told him the city I was in but she didn't tell him *where* I was. I always found him before he found me. She gave me as much of a head start as she could. I can't blame her for that."

"I can." Mountain sneered.

Melora shook her head. Then asked, "Have you ever had one special person in your life? That one person who held you when you were scared, who dried your tears and didn't laugh at you when you did something you knew better than to do? The one person who cared about you when you gave up on yourself? That person for me is Izzy and I hope I mean as much to her. If you can't forgive her, then you can't forgive me. That's just the way it is."

Mountain snapped his mouth closed. Her words slammed into him. He didn't understand them. Izzy had betrayed her time and time again, yet she was willing to overlook her misdeeds. Suddenly, he couldn't wait to meet this woman. As much as he knew he wouldn't do it, he wanted to slam his fist into her mouth. His daddy taught him never to hit a woman but he was tempted in this instance. "I can't wait to meet her." He growled.

Melora grinned. "I can't wait to see her again. You guys are gonna love her."

"Not bloody likely," Mountain whispered.

Chapter Nine

By late afternoon, everyone was awake and there had been some progress on locating Whiskey. He'd been moving around the city all day and the guys from Redemption House had been following him every step of the way.

Melora was tired of being cooped up in the clubhouse though. The four walls were closing in on her.

Cassie came up to her and asked, "Is there anything I can get you?"

Melora shook her head. "I'm fine."

Cassie laughed. "No you're not. You're as wired as a ticking bomb."

Melora smiled. "How did you know?"

"I recognize the look in your eyes." Cassie nodded with a knowing look in her eyes. "When I feel that way, I paint. It relieves the stress and I can calm down."

"Yeah, well I don't paint." Melora shrugged.

"So what do you do?"

Melora shrugged. She wasn't ready to share her secret yet.

Cassie grabbed her hand and led her to a quiet corner. Sitting down with Melora she asked, "What do you do? We all have our stress releaser. No one here is going to judge you."

Melora took a deep breath. No one but Izzy knew about her hobby and as much as she wanted to keep her secret, she knew she couldn't. She had to find some release. "I write."

"Really?" Cassie smiled. "That's great. I wish I could do that. Do you have anything published yet?"

Melora nodded. "Yeah I do. I write under a pen name." She turned to Cassie. "Please don't tell anyone. I don't want anyone else to know."

"I won't, I promise," Cassie vowed. "Tell me what you need."

"Just a space away from everyone else. I have a laptop, I just need some alone space."

"How about if you go down to our house?" Cassie asked. "It's not far and still inside the compound."

"That would be great." Melora felt the stress flow away from her body at the suggestion.

"Good, then let me tell Deke where we're going and we'll get moving." Cassie got to her feet and walked over to her husband.

Melora hoped she would be able to go by herself. She hated someone hovering over her shoulder. But she would survive this, she always did. She went to the bedroom and retrieved her backpack. Inside was everything she needed. She went back to the bench and waited for Cassie.

Cassie returned and held out her hand. Melora took it and walked behind her as they both left the clubhouse. "I told Deke you were coming to the house to get some rest, away from everyone else. That should buy you a couple of hours anyway."

Melora nodded. "That would be great."

"So what do you write?"

Melora fingered the strap of her backpack. "Mostly romance with a little mystery."

Cassie grinned. "My favorite kind. Are you strictly a PG writer or do you do the real thing?"

Melora blushed. "The real thing I guess."

Cassie laughed. "Good. I love a book I can believe in. Can't wait to read you one day."

Melora felt her cheeks flush with warmth. When they went into the house, she found herself under another gaze.

The woman she guessed was Peaches stood in the kitchen getting a drink of water. She raised her finger to her lips. "I just got the little heathens down for their naps."

Cassie grinned. "Your son Jesse Junior may be a heathen but my kids are angels."

"Yeah right, they take after their mother." Peaches shook her head. "Face it woman, they are all heathens but we love them anyway."

"That's true enough." Cassie agreed. "This is Melora and she's here to rest. I'm putting her in the library for a while."

"Best place there is to catch some quiet. I'm Peaches as you might have guessed." Peaches grinned. "I'll just get my book and let you have the peace."

"What are you reading?" Cassie asked.

"The latest book from our favorite author, Delanie Shane."

"Oh good, I want to read it after you. I love that girl." Cassie grinned.

Melora felt a flush of pride inside. How small a world is that? She was Delanie Shane and these women loved her writing? It made her feel so good. For the first time in years, she felt a little beam of light. Maybe this was the right place for her to be for a while.

"So how is the story coming along? Did Harry ever get to second base with Olivia?" Cassie asked.

Peaches nodded. "Second base and a whole lot further." She sighed. "But I wish she would finish the story of Greg and Tammy. I loved that story and hated to see it end."

"Yeah, she did leave us hanging on that one," Cassie agreed. "Maybe she'll do another book about them."

"I hope so, while I love all her characters, those two are my favorite. They get into so much trouble it's almost funny." Peaches sighed. "Ok, on to better things while the heathens sleep."

Melora watched as she made her way to the next room. "So you guys like this author? Maybe I should read her work."

Cassie laughed. "Honey, we love this girl. She does get into the best kind of trouble sometimes. Her stories are funny and so true to life. I can almost believe I'm one of her characters. I love that in an author."

Peaches returned and Melora went into the library. Closing the door behind her, she thought about what the two other women had suggested. They felt the Greg and Tammy story needed a little something more huh? Well, she would see what she could do about that. In fact, she had a great idea what would happen next in their saga.

Hurrying over to the desk, she got her minicomputer out and put in her flash drive. There were seven files on the drive but each file had several subfiles in it. She clicked on the Greg and Tammy file. Three different books came up. Clicking on the blurbs file, she reviewed the short blurb for each book. Then she sat back in her chair and thought about a new plot for a moment. Then suddenly, she smiled. The most devious plot just popped into her mind.

She opened her word file and got busy. Her fingers flew over the keys as thought after thought crossed her mind. A couple of hours later, she finally came out of her stupor when she heard a knock on the door. She quickly saved everything she'd written and was simply amazed at her progress. "Come in," she called out softly.

Cassie's head popped through the open doorway. "How is it going in here?'

Melora grinned. "It's going."

"Good. I just got a call from Deke. They want you back in the clubhouse."

Melora quickly closed up her computer and slid the flash drive into her pocket. "I'm ready to go back." She paused and added, "Thank you for this afternoon. I needed this time away badly."

"I don't know what's going on up at the clubhouse but something is about to happen," Cassie informed her as she came into the room. "Deke's voice had a tone in it that I didn't like."

"Oh, crap." Melora sighed heavily. "Now what? What else can go wrong?"

"We'd better find out before the shit hits the fan."

"Okay, let's go and see what the next disaster is." Melora packed up her computer and drew the back over her shoulder. Together, they walked back to the clubhouse and into a shouting match.

Deke, Gator, Sam, Iceman and Mountain sat on one side while an unidentified man sat on the other side of the table. All six men were yelling at one another.

Melora stood there a moment and shook her head. Lifting her fingers to her mouth, she let loose a sharp ear piercing whistle that stopped all the noise as everyone in the room cringed at the sound. "Just what the bloody hell is going on here?" she asked.

All the men just glared at her.

"Woman...this is a MC, not a fraternity. You don't disrespect us like that." Deke growled.

"You all sound more like school boys arguing over something rather stupid than an MC." She scolded. "And before you say it, I know you're all big bad asses, so just quit." She looked at the newest member at the club. "Who is he?"

Sam walked over to her and whispered, "He's Senator Walker. He got your message and came to meet you in person." He turned to the group standing at the table. "We were just discussing that very thing."

The newcomer stiffened as he glared at her. "I'm told you have evidence that someone other than yourself murdered my nephew. What is this evidence? I demand to see it at once."

Melora snorted. "You can demand all you want but until you ask me nicely, I don't have to show you squat."

There were multiple gasps in the room as the silence settled.

"Excuse me?" Senator Walker sneered.

"No I don't think I will." Melora shook her head.

"Baby, maybe you should reconsider," Sam urged. "He's an important guy."

"Why?" Melora turned her head to study him. "This asshat puts his pants on one leg at a time just like we do. Why should his lack of manners do anything to me? I know I didn't kill Baily and I know I can prove it. Why should I bow to him?"

Senator Walker scowled. "Show me the proof."

Melora shook her head. "You may be a big man in Washington but you aren't in Washington right now. Ask me without demanding and I will show you what happened that night. All I'm asking for is the respect you seem to demand but don't show to others."

Senator Paul Walker took a deep breath. His face was still flush but he exhaled loudly as he seemed to calm down and asked, "Can you prove you didn't kill Baily?"

"Yes, I can." Melora walked over to where he was standing and took out her phone. Bringing up the video, she played it for him.

Paul Walker frowned as the video played out. Then he looked around the room. "So Baily is really dead and has been all along?" His face had paled.

Each man there nodded. They'd all seen the video and they knew the truth.

Walker turned back to Melora. "He told me you killed Baily and he even offered to find out where the body was hidden. Now, I know I'll never recover him. I'll never be able to bring closure for his mother."

"You will," Melora stated quietly.

"How so?" Paul asked.

"Because the hogs never got near Baily's body that night."

Paul frowned. "But you heard what he said."

"Yes I did, but what Whiskey doesn't know is I moved Baily's body before the hogs got there. Only I know where he actually is."

"And where is that?"

Melora shook her head. "I'll only tell you after Whiskey is dead and I no longer have this murder charge hanging over my head."

"Is it really true Whiskey wants to run guns and drugs on the East coast and he was going to use a connection to me to do it?" Senator Walker asked.

"Yes, it's true."

Walker looked over at Raven and shook his head. "That man is insane if he thinks I'll let that happen."

Raven snorted. "He thinks he's gonna take the club away from me as well."

He turned to Deke and asked, "What can I do to help you guys stop him?"

"Just stay out of our way. We'll take care of the man and his friends."

Senator Walker nodded. Looking at Raven again, he commented, "Let me know when he's neutralized. I don't want to know when or how." He turned back to Melora. "I would like to know where Baily's body is after this is over. He deserves a proper burial and my sister deserves closure in this matter."

"I promise I'll let you know."

He turned to the room at large and announced, "Gentlemen, I'll be leaving now. I hope to hear you have this matter in hand and I expect results soon." He then walked to the door and left.

A few minutes later, they heard a helicopter start up and take off.

Deke turned to Melora. Then he crooked a finger in her direction.

She stepped closer.

"Don't ever do that again. I will not tolerate disrespect in my clubhouse."

Melora nodded. "I really didn't show you any disrespect. At least, I don't think I did. The only disrespect I saw was from the Senator. But I am sorry if you feel I did that."

"She's got a valid point," Gator spoke up. "He didn't seem to respect us at all."

Melora held up her hands. "Before this starts another argument, let's drop it. I apologize." She turned to Sam. "That takes care of one of the problems, now we just have to stop Whiskey. Does anyone know where he is at the moment?"

"He and his boys are roaming the city looking for you," Raven answered. "BTW thanks for putting Mr. Bigshot in his place. I was about ready to floor him myself. With my fist down his throat." He swung his gaze over at Deke. "Of course, this is your town and I respect that, so I didn't follow my instincts this time." He gave Deke a grin.

Deke stared back at him with an emotionless expression.

"People like him give people like you guy's bad names." Melora smiled. "I know he won't remember today but I feel better about it."

"Oh, I don't think he'll forget what you did to him. He's just happy no one but us saw it." Iceman snickered.

Melora glanced over at Raven. "Are you and me okay? I don't want any trouble with your MC over this."

Raven shook his head. "We're okay. None of this was ever your fault. I know that now. Whiskey is the traitor and I plan to bring the hammer down on him myself."

"As much as I deplore violence I can't wait for him to get his." Melora shuddered. "He wanted blood, but it's gonna be his own spilt and not mine."

"Don't you worry about that." Raven seethed. "He won't live long enough to worry too much about it."

"That's good enough for me." Melora gazed into his eyes as she spoke.

~****~

Mountain walked over to Melora and asked, "Can we talk?"

She nodded. "I think maybe we should. Time is running out and there's so much you and I need to talk about before it's too late."

Taking her elbow, he led her away from the others. Taking a seat in the far corner, he stared at her for a moment then asked, "I want to know if you'll come back with us when we leave. Come back to Texas with us I mean. I'd like the chance to know you better and we've been gone long enough now."

Melora stared at him for a long moment. "I don't know. When this is over, I just want to get on with my life."

Mountain looked away then glanced back at her. "But if you don't have a job anywhere yet, what would it hurt to come and stay with me for a while?"

Melora shrugged. "I don't yet know what I want to do. Maybe I'll stay here, maybe I'll move on to another place. I just don't know."

"Can you at least think about it?" he asked. "We've missed out on everything so far, I don't want to miss out on the rest of your life."

"I guess we'll have to wait and see what happens over the next few days." Melora shrugged. "Who knows if either of us will live through this."

Mountain glared. "The only one who's going to die will be Whiskey."

Melora laid her hand on his arm and shook her head. "No one can predict the future, not even this one." She laughed without mirth. "I can only hope to survive the next few days but otherwise, I can't make plans of any kind right now. I'm sorry."

"Will you at least think about it?"

Melora nodded. "That I will do." She got to her feet. "But right now we have to come up with a plan that ensures safety for everyone but Whiskey." She walked back to the main table and began listening to the others talk.

Mountain watched her for a moment then got up and walked down the hall to the room he had. When he closed the door, he went to his bag and sat down on the bed. From inside the leather saddlebag he pulled out an envelope. Inside were the papers the lawyer had given him four years ago. The letter from Carla and the DNA test that claimed Melora was his daughter. He knew without the test that she was his child, yet even with this knowledge, he couldn't get through to her.

He wanted nothing more than to know her as a person, yet she wouldn't allow him to do that. Mountain knew he had to find a way to get through to her. He needed to find a way to understand her, so he could know what was in her heart. He wasn't going to give up on the only thing in his life that was truly his. *His daughter.*

Chapter Ten

The afternoon melted into evening and with the night came a peace only the darkness could bring. It also brought the shadows that could hide evil but this night no evil could be found around the compound.

Sometime after midnight, when most everyone had gone to bed, only Sam, Mountain, Deke, Gator and Melora were sitting there in the great room when they heard the sound of bikes coming closer.

At first, the whine of the bikes didn't phase Melora but as the sound got closer her head suddenly snapped up. She turned fearfully toward the front door as sweat beaded on her forehead. Getting quickly to her feet, the chair she was sitting on slid out from underneath her and she backed away.

Sam watched her action. He looked toward his son and Deke frowned.

Mountain stared at her for a moment then turned toward the sound of the bikes coming closer.

Gator and Deke stomped toward the door while Sam went to Melora and wrapped his arms around her shoulders.

Mountain stood in front of them with his weapon in his hand ready for anything.

Then the sounds of the bikes stopped outside the main gate. The noise dimmed for a moment as the trio sitting on the massive bikes sat there staring into the compound.

Deke and Gator stood in the open doorway and with the lights from the clubhouse behind them, they seemed more like shadows than the imposing men they both were.

Whiskey, Micah and Lightning revved their engines but came no closer. Only the locked gate kept them away. One by one, the men making rounds inside the gates came into view. The bikers could see the rifles in their hands and no one on the other side of the fence made a move toward their own weapons. Instead, they twisted their throttles on their handlebars to make the engines rev louder.

After a few minutes, Whiskey gave them a salute and they turned their bikes and roared off into the darkness.

Deke and Gator watched as the night swallowed them, then turned and went back inside.

Deke grabbed the bottle of Black Velvet on the table and poured a drink. Slamming it back, he brought his cold gaze up to Melora. "I think he knows where you are."

Melora turned her face into Sam's chest. His arms tightened around her but it didn't seem to help. The cold wrapping itself around her, holding onto her soul became deeper and she couldn't seem to stop it. She couldn't stop herself from shivering either. "Oh God, he's going to kill me, I can feel it," she whimpered against Sam's throat.

"No baby, he won't even get close to you," Sam whispered into her hair.

"You can't say that. He found me again."

"Well, you did tell him where you were," Mountain reminded her.

Melora shook her head. "No, I told him I was in Troy, not where I was staying. I never mentioned I was here in the clubhouse."

"She's got a point." Deke noted as he lifted his head. "How did they know where she was? Troy is a good sized city and they haven't been here long enough to search the whole city. They didn't have time to figure out she was here."

"So how did they pinpoint her location so quickly?" Mountain asked.

No one could give him an answer.

"I think we should try and get some sleep. We can figure out whatever is going on in the morning," Sam suggested.

"Sounds like a plan." Deke sighed. "We all need to sleep to be on top of our game tomorrow."

Mountain turned and went down the hall to his room without saying a word.

Sam led Melora to the room they shared. Once he closed the door he said, "I think you need to forgive him."

Melora sat down on the bed and looked at him. "Forgive who?"

"Your dad." Sam nodded. "He just wants the chance to know you."

"Yeah, well I've got other things to worry about right now. He can wait."

Sam knelt in front of her. "Honey, I know your life is a mess right now but here's the thing...that man is a part of you, he'll always be a part of you. He wants to get to know you since he never got the chance before. He'll do whatever he has to in order for that to happen. I know how he feels, baby, I didn't know about Deke until he was twelve. I felt lost when he came to live with me and I made some pretty big mistakes in his regard. But I got a second chance and I'm still here. I know what you're going through is scary but you need to know you aren't alone in this situation. It isn't just you against the whole world any more. You got a lot of people behind you now and you've got the truth as well." He paused then ran his fingers through his hair. "I have no idea why we're together but we are. I think you need to let your dad in too. At least give him a chance."

Melora placed her hand against his cheek. "When we hooked up, I wasn't looking for a father figure. I needed more than that. I needed you. You weren't about that, okay?" Shrugging she continued, "You can't miss what you never had. Mountain wasn't there for me and my mom and that's okay. It was his choice to ride away. Who knows if he would have been there for us even if he had known about me? When this is over, I'll make the time to know him but he has to make a choice as well. He has to let the past be and accept me, as I am today, not look at me as a child. I'm a full grown woman now."

Sam chuckled. "I think we've got that established. You most certainly are full grown and I love your body."

"Then come use me, make me forget at least for a little while that there's someone out there that wants to kill me." Melora whispered as her lips touched his.

Sam groaned and surged forward carrying her backwards. He lifted her and set her down in the middle of the bed. Reaching up, he removed her wig, allowing her silken strands to fall over her shoulders. He gazed intently at her halo of hair as he took a satiny strand and rubbed it between his fingers. "My silk girl," he whispered hoarsely.

Melora grinned. "Woman," she reminded him.

He chuckled again. "Nah, I like Silk Girl better."

She stared into his eyes. "Why do they call you Bones?" she asked as she raised his t-shirt sleeve and smoothed a finger over his skull tattoo.

Sam raised a brow and shrugged. "Over the years, I've crushed a lot of them."

Melora tilted her head in confusion. "A lot of what?"

He laughed. "Bones, *silk woman*...bones." Then he crushed her lips with his. His hands then literally ripped her clothes off. When her shirt and bra were gone, his mouth closed over her nipple. His teeth bit down and he suckled it deep into his mouth.

Melora whimpered.

The only thing between him and her core was the tiny triangle of her silk underwear covering her mound. His mouth slid down along her body until he was right where he wanted to be. He pulled her panties to the side and spread her folds using his tongue to lap at her.

Sam groaned when he felt her wet heat. It was almost pulsing in its intensity while his tongue swiped at her sweet skin. Her unique taste drove him wild and he groaned as her essence flooded his mouth.

When he couldn't contain himself any longer he ripped the fabric left between them and his fingers fumbled with his own clothes. Kicking his jeans off, he settled between her open thighs and rammed his hard hot cock into her.

He paused and waited as he felt himself surrounded by her tight sheath. If he wasn't careful, he would lose himself in her heat before he was ready. He didn't know why but when he was with her he felt like a damn kid again.

He began to move slowly inside her but she wasn't going to let him. Thrust after thrust, she lifted her hips to meet his and before long, Sam lost it. He began to thrust harder and faster and a moment before he came, he felt her come apart in his arms. She screamed out his name as his lips came down on hers. His mouth muffled her screams somewhat but not entirely.

Moving to her side, he wrapped his arms around her and brought her close. He snuggled closer when he felt her trembling. "Are you okay?" he whispered.

Melora laughed out loud. "Not really. I have never climaxed that hard before. What kind of magic do you have, *Bones*?"

Sam chuckled. "I don't know about the magic, but when it's right between two people, it's just right. I guess it's right between us, huh?"

~******~

Melora closed her eyes and let her body relax. She didn't answer him, she couldn't seem to speak. In his arms, she did feel safe and that was a good feeling. For most of her life since her mother died, she hadn't felt this safe. She began to drift away into the sweet depths of sleep, with her head resting on his chest while she listened to the sound of his heartbeat.

A few hours later, a soft knock woke them. Sam got up and grabbing his jeans, he answered the door.

Melora heard them speaking but she didn't really pay any attention. When he came back over to the bed and knelt beside it, she opened her eyes. Turning her head, she noted it was still dark outside. "What's up?"

"Deke needs you to identify a woman claiming to be Izzy."

Melora's eyes widened. Sitting up, she cried out, "Izzy is here?" Grabbing her clothes, she dressed in a hurry and rushed out.

When she came into the main room, she saw her friend sitting at a table with a couple of the guys standing there. "Izzy!" Melora cried out as she rushed toward her.

Beaming, Izzy got to her feet and waited for Melora to reach her.

Wrapping her arms around her friend Melora hugged her close. Tears ran down her cheeks as she stepped back a pace and searched her friend's face. She saw the fading bruises and the haunted look in her friend's eyes. "Oh, my god—I'm so sorry," she whispered. "I never meant for you to get caught up in this."

Izzy grabbed her arms hard and shook her. "Don't you dare take this away from him. This was never your fault."

Melora sat down with her. "But it was my fault. I put you in his line of fire." She swallowed hard. "I never meant to involve you."

Izzy held out her hand and cupped Melora's cheek. "I know that and you didn't. I knew when I got home that night and found you missing...something bad was going down. Then a few days later, Whiskey and his friend came for me but as soon as he told me what was going on, I knew he wasn't telling the truth. I knew you wouldn't kill someone, not for money or power. Whiskey lied to save his own hide. Everything that happened in the last two years is on Whiskey. The little bastard thought no one would care about me. He told me often enough that I was expendable and no one would care whether I was dead or alive. I tried to tell him he didn't know you very well if that's what he thought but all he could do was laugh at me."

Melora's eyes narrowed. "Yeah, that is going to be his last mistake."

"Melora, I take it this is your friend Izzy," Deke suggested.

She looked up and noticed everyone standing around them. "Oh, I'm so sorry." She got to her feet. "Yes, this is my best friend, Izzy Zackery."

Izzy got to her feet and faced them. "My name is Isabell Zackery. I know you all probably think I've betrayed my best friend but I didn't. For the longest time, we were all the other one had. I would never betray that."

"But you let Whiskey and his friends know where she was time and time again." Mountain crossed his arms over his chest. "Why would you do that and not call it betrayal?"

Izzy shook her head. "I may have been forced to tell them what city she was in but I never told them where in the city she was. She always picked the bigger cities, so they had to search for her. I couldn't give her much but I could give her that. A head start and a warning."

"Too bad, it took me two years to catch on to that fact," Melora muttered.

Izzy let out a deep breath and asked, "So now what? Does Whiskey know you're here?"

Melora nodded. "Yeah, he found me last night."

Izzy paled and sat down. "I was afraid of that."

"What do you mean?" Sam asked.

Izzy pushed the hair out of her eyes. "It means Whiskey has someone else watching out for him. When Silas came to pick him up the other night, Jonesy made a quick phone call. I didn't hear who he called but he did tell them he was found out. He said it was up to him now. Then he turned to me and sneered that we both would be dead soon and justice would be theirs."

"So Whiskey has someone else waiting in the background huh?" Sam almost grinned as if he wanted to break some more bones. He turned to Izzy. "How do we find this rat?"

Izzy shrugged. "I don't know but Whiskey has more than one member in his back pocket. He liked to brag about if he were in charge, they'd all make better money and have no troubles with the law. He always said the law worked for those who paid the most for its protection. Some of the other Ghosts believe that too and they aren't afraid to break the laws to get what they want."

"So, what all did he find out about Melora? Through you I mean?" Sam asked.

Izzy and Melora glared at him. "I didn't tell him anything about her, other than what city she said she was in," Izzy argued hotly.

"Stop it." Mountain growled as he paced. "We aren't going to get anywhere when everyone is arguing about her involvement. Now we have to put our anger aside and work to come up with a plan to get to Whiskey."

"You may not believe me and I don't care one way or the other." Izzy looked around and stared especially at Mountain, then she turned to Melora. "As long as you believe me the rest of them can go to hell. I would never betray you girl. You've had my back for so long I can't imagine my life without you in it. I would never betray that." Tears rolled down her cheeks.

"I know, believe me I know," Melora told her. "I would never betray you either."

"So now all we have to do is figure out who is working with Whiskey on the inside before he comes after Melora," Deke stated.

"It isn't going to be easy to get to her now." Sam pointed out. "She's safe as long as she's behind these walls."

"Let's hope so." Mountain nodded.

"How can they get to her here?" Deke asked.

Mountain stood tall and glared at Deke, Gator and Sam. "I will do what I have to do to protect my daughter, even if you guys don't agree. I won't put anyone else in danger but I will not let them get to her."

Izzy gasped as she turned to Melora. "Daughter? What is he talking about?"

Melora grimaced. "Izzy, meet the man who fathered me twenty four years ago."

Izzy turned and searched Mountain's face. She noted the white hair his violet eyes, the hint of a strong chin and the dimple in his cheek. Then she turned to her friend. "And how do you feel about this?"

Melora shrugged. "I haven't really had time to think about it. He..." She jerked her thumb at him. "...Seems to think it makes a difference but I haven't made up my mind yet. I never thought about him all this time and now, he thinks he has some sort of say in how I live my life."

"You already know the reason I didn't come around before. I didn't know about you until four years ago." Mountain growled. "Then I had to find you. With the way you have moved around, no wonder I couldn't."

"Let's not do this again." Sam protested. "Look it's a new day, maybe we should concentrate on Whiskey for now."

Then Raven and his men came into the room along with Mountain's men. As the room filled up, everyone heard Reva and a few others in the kitchen. Before long coffee and pancakes were being served.

Izzy just happened to glance up at the same time one of Raven's men came out of the kitchen. As he was holding a cup of coffee and a plate of food, she stared at him. A few minutes' later, plates of pancakes were laid in front of them.

Everyone dug into their breakfast. Melora closed her eyes as she took a bit of her pancakes. She loved pancakes, then a moment later, her eyes widened and she stumbled backwards. Her chair flew out from under her and she grabbed her throat.

"OMG, what's going on?" Reva shouted as she rushed forward.

When Melora dropped to the floor, Sam, Mountain and Izzy were by her side.

Deke, Gator Raven and the others all stood around and watched. They all felt helpless.

"What the fuck is happening?" Sam growled as he helplessly watched her struggle to breathe. She was hyperventilating just to get air into her lungs.

Mountain watched as her face paled and her lips began to turn blue. He looked as helpless as Sam. It was Izzy who finally said, "I've only seen her do this once. She inhaled some peanut dust. She's very allergic to peanuts." She began going through Melora's pockets and found a small package of Benadryl. Breaking open the package she pushed the medicine into her mouth but her throat was so swollen she couldn't swallow. "Damn it, does anyone have an EpiPen?" Izzy screamed. "She needs an EpiPen. She'll die without it!"

Mountain reached inside his cut and brought out a small, white plastic cylinder. Flipping open the cover, he slammed the pen down on her thigh. The click of the pen injecting the medicine inside her seemed to echo in the room.

They all waited anxiously. The rasping of Melora's labored breathing was the only sound in the room.

A moment later, the blue began to fade from Melora's lips and her breathing eased.

Izzy pulled her up onto her lap and rocked her back and forth. Tears ran down her face as she held her friend. "God, don't scare me like that girl," she whispered. "Don't do that ever again!"

Melora choked out a chuckle. "I'll try. It hurts too much." Her voice was barely above a whisper. Looking up at Izzy she asked, "Where did you get the Epi from? The only one I had ran out about six months ago."

Izzy glanced over at Mountain. "I didn't have any, he did."

Melora slowly turned her head to stare at her father. "Why did you have one?" she asked softly.

Mountain stared at her for a moment. "I have the same allergy you do. I've learned to always have one on my person somewhere."

"Well, ain't that a kick in the head," she whispered as she stared at the man who shared more than blood with her.

"What I want to know is why you would eat peanuts with such a violent allergy to them?" Sam asked with concern in his voice.

Melora shook her head. "I wouldn't. Not on purpose anyway."

Mountain and Deke got up and stared at her plate of food.

Deke took a knife and separated the two pancakes on the plate. Between the pancakes was a layer of fine powder. Licking his finger, he dipped into the powder and brought it to his lips. He stared at Mountain for a moment then turned to Melora and the others. "Well, someone knows you have an allergy, they put ground nuts between your pancakes."

Melora gasped and Izzy echoed it.

Sam reached down and helped her to her feet. Wrapping his arms around her, he held her for a moment then assisted her to a chair.

Reva had come to take away her plate and Izzy poured her some fresh coffee.

"Damn." Melora swore as her hands shook while setting her cup down.

Izzy dropped to her knees next to where she sat. "I didn't do this," she whispered to her friend.

Melora raised her hand to cup her friend's cheek. "Damn, Izzy...I know that!"

Izzy closed her eyes. "But they don't. They think I tried to kill you."

Melora looked up to the faces of the men around her. She could see Izzy was right. Everyone was staring at Izzy with more than questions in their eyes.

"Did you mention this allergy to anyone in Whiskey's camp?" Deke asked.

Izzy started to shake her head then remembered something. "I don't think so but one night when Whiskey was there they were all drinking and doing dope when someone mentioned snacks. Jonesy got up and brought some peanuts to the table. When I didn't eat any Whiskey tried to force me to eat with them but I didn't want any. I tried to stop him but I couldn't. I spit them out and Whiskey got mad, screamed at me that I was wasting good food and I said I didn't eat nuts of any kind. I told him I wouldn't have them in the house. I think he knew the reason was because my roommate was allergic but I swear I didn't tell them that."

"Okay, so who here would know that?" Raven asked. He'd been shaken by what happened. He'd never seen anyone suffer something like that. In his life, people died sometimes by violence or old age but never like that. He searched the faces of the men he'd brought with him. They too were shaken by what happened. Then he spotted Gremlin. He was the only one who wasn't all that shaken. He tipped his head and continued to study the other man.

When Gremlin noticed his gaze, he met Raven's eyes with a steady look.

Raven growled. He couldn't prove it but he knew Gremlin was Whiskey's inside man. "Why?" he asked. "Why did you do it?"

Gremlin looked around. "What are you talking about man? I didn't do anything!"

Raven scoffed. "Yeah, you did. You ground up a few peanuts and slipped them into her food." He stormed over to face the other man. "What did Whiskey promise you? What did he give you to betray this club?"

Gremlin stumbled to his feet. "I don't have any idea what you're talking about man. This club is everything to me!"

Raven grabbed the other man's shirt and hauled him closer. "You bastard. You damn near killed someone, doesn't that mean anything to you? She's an innocent. We don't kill innocents."

Gremlin sneered but didn't say anything.

Raven shoved the other man back down in his chair. Then he turned to stare at the rest of his men. "I'm only going to say this one time. The Ghosts of Dixie is my club and yours but this is beyond what the club stands for. We are not murderers and thieves, we are a motorcycle club not a band of thugs. If I do find out that one of my own is responsible for this, I will gladly hand them over to Deke and Mountain. Right now, we're a strong influence in our town, under Whiskey's rule you'll be out running from the law every single day. He's so far gone, you won't be able to trust him. He's ruled by the dope he should've been smart enough to avoid in the first god damn place. He planned to take over the club, then run guns and dope up and down the east coast. Do any of you guys think he's above the laws of this land? Do any of you guys want to become outlaws? Do you think you'll really be safe if he takes over the club?"

"Hell, Whiskey would put a bullet in your head for looking at him wrong and you guys know it." Chase scoffed. Chase was one of Mountain's men.

"He ambushed Travis when he was going back to his motel room," Rigger, another of Mountain's men, stated. "He stood in the shadows and waited for Travis to pass him before he shot him in the back." Rigger got to his feet and stared at the men Raven brought with him. "And do you want to know why he did it? Because Travis stopped him from beating a woman who spilled a drink on the table, he was sitting at. She didn't spill it on him, just the damn table. She didn't deserve to be hit for that but Whiskey didn't care. He put a bullet in Travis's back and now, he'll never walk again. Hell, he almost didn't live but Travis had a strong will. He survived the bullet but he'll never play with his kids again, and he'll never make love to his woman again. That's what your precious Whiskey does and will do again!"

"He isn't going to get the chance," Mountain vowed. "You may not know or care but this girl is my kid, any threat to her is a threat to my club and we will not tolerate it." He joined Raven and stared at his men. "If you allow Whiskey to get to her, be prepared to go to war with the Sons of Satan. We will bring the full wrath down on your heads and no one will survive." Then he turned and went back to Melora's side. He stood beside Sam, placed his hands on her shoulders and glared at the others.

One by one, his men came to stand beside him.

Then one by one, they *all* came to stand behind their leaders.

Chapter Eleven

Later in the day, Mountain finally caught up with his daughter. The clubhouse was almost empty. Melora stood at the back door watching the men make their rounds outside.

"Are you all right?" he asked.

Melora nodded and turned to glance at him. "Thanks to you I'm alive." She looked away and licked her dry lips. "Do you really think one of Raven's men put ground peanuts in my food?"

"Yeah, I do and I think Raven was right about who did it."

Shaking her head, she whispered, "Wow, I've never had anyone hate me like this before."

"Whiskey won't get close to you." Mountain shook his head.

Melora laid her hand on his arm. "You don't know that. You can threaten all you want but he'll use anyone and anything he needs to get what he wants. Even though at this point everyone knows the truth, he won't stop until I'm dead. "

"He knows it's too late."

Melora scoffed. "At this point that idea is moot. Now he knows he's got nothing left to lose. I'm sure Gremlin told him Walker was here."

"Then he knows he lost everything."

"Yeah, but he's gonna make sure I pay for sticking my nose in his business." She sighed deeply. "I guess I knew this day was coming ever since that day in Raleigh. I hoped to just slip away and turn up somewhere else, safe and sound."

Mountain stared at her for a moment then had to ask, "Why didn't you do that then?"

Melora shrugged. "Well, I intended to, but Sam made me turn and face it. And maybe I was tired of letting the bad guy win every Goddamn time." Her voice was low. "When it all came out...I finally found my courage again. I didn't want to let this go on anymore. Baily didn't deserve what happened to him that night either. He was stupid to cross Raven and Whiskey but he didn't deserve to die like that. Not over something so inconsequential as money. "

Mountain rolled his eyes. "Not everyone thinks money is inconsequential."

Melora shrugged. "Not everyone is hung up on the almighty buck either. Having lived with little or less than little money, I just don't see the draw to it."

"Sometimes it's all that matters to some people."

"I know and for them all I can feel is pity."

"Pity? Why?"

"There's so much out there that money can't buy, like a brilliant sunrise or sunset. Like the beauty of nature at its finest, or like the feeling of love's first kiss. Or the way having a best friend can make the day better. All those things in life are more important to me than money."

Mountain was quiet for a moment then said, "I'm sorry you and your mom had it so rough when you were little. If I'd known about you I would have come back for you."

Melora shook her head. "She wouldn't have wanted that. She loved you enough in the week you two were together to let you go in the end." Shrugging she admitted, "We had what we needed even if it wasn't always a lot. We had each other and that was enough. She taught me more in the ten years I had her than I learned after she was gone."

"Can I ask you why you're with the old man?" His hands fisted.

Melora touched his forearm. "It isn't because I was looking for a father figure." Her words were low. "Like I told Sam, you can't miss what you never had. I went to Sam because I wanted him. I'd never needed a man before him but that night, I needed *him*. I never had the urge to share myself with a man before I met him. Mom always told me to save my body for a worthy man. A man who I felt deserved my love. I don't know if I feel love for Sam or even if he feels it for me but right now, it feels right being with him. I hope you can understand that."

Her words shocked Mountain. He stared at her for a moment then tried to say something but no words came out of his mouth.

Melora chuckled softly "Yes, I was a virgin before Sam and I don't make any excuses for that. In fact, I'm proud of it."

"So am I," Mountain admitted. "Carla was a virgin the night we met too. I never told anyone about her because I wasn't willing to share what we had together with anyone. But I think you need to know what your mother and I had together. I never had a relationship after her either. Nothing that lasted." After a moment or so he asked, "So what are you going to do after this situation is over?"

Melora shrugged. "I have no clue. I've been running for so long, I don't have any plans for the future. I haven't been able to make any plans and I won't be able to until Whiskey is dead or I am." She hesitated then added, "I'm hoping we get the chance to have that talk about you and Mom. She was a special woman."

"You won't be dead." Mountain growled.

"I do know that I'm tired of living on this ledge I find myself on." She glared out at the yard and the fence. "I'm tired of looking over my shoulder all the time and I'm tired of being scared all the time."

"We need to end this soon," her father said.

Just then, Cassie and Peaches joined them. "Come for a walk with us," Cassie offered. "I need to use up some energy and I imagine you do too. We're safe as long as we're inside the compound."

Mountain looked troubled. "I'll come with you."

Melora smiled. "Down boy! I need breathing space. I'm kind of tired of the male kind right now." She turned to gaze at Cassie and Peaches. "I would love to walk with you." Hooking both her arms in theirs.

Mountain turned and stomped in through the back door.

The women all laughed softly.

"Dammed Alpha bikers," Peaches joked.

The three women laughed.

"Yep, just like in the books," Cassie added with a laugh. "Throwing their weight around all the freakin time."

"Wait a damn minute!" Deke called from the door.

Cassie sighed and turned her head toward her husband. "We will be alright. It's just a woman thing. We need to have that, ok?"

His eyes narrowed at her.

"And please don't send a posse after us, we will be right here in the compound. Please?" Her voice sounded sweet and soft.

Deke grunted while looking worried as the women walked away, arm in arm.

They left the clubhouse and began walking the perimeter of the compound.

They were quiet for a while but then Peaches burst out, "So you and Bones, what's that all about?"

Melora chuckled. "Why is that all everyone is concerned about? Me and Sam? What's so strange about it?"

"Well, the man is older than dirt." Cassie laughed.

Melora chuckled. "Yeah, he is older but he's also a beautiful human being. And he's very sexy."

Peaches chuckled. "Yeah, he is. If I wasn't with Iceman I would admire him. I mean I do admire him but not that way."

Cassie chuckled. "That's a good thing, Iceman doesn't do competition."

Peaches grinned and sighed. "Yeah, I know but he's a beautiful Alpha human being too."

All three girls chuckled. "I think all three of us got lucky," Cassie admitted. She glanced over at Melora. "You not only found Sam but also your father."

Melora stumbled. Sighing heavily, she admitted, "Yeah that's weird."

"Why?" Peaches asked.

Melora just shook her head. "I don't know, I guess I never thought about him much. I had no one, then now I got a man and a dad? My Mom used to tell me about him when I was small but I haven't thought about him in so long, I guess I forgot he existed. Now he's here and he thinks he can tell me what to do. It's just new to me."

"I think it's sweet," Peaches told them. "But I can see what you're saying. After I got back with my father and grandfather they too, tried to tell me what I could do." Shrugging, she continued, "It took them a while to get used to the fact I was grown up. I wasn't the little girl I was the last time they saw me."

Suddenly, the quiet around them was shattered by the sound of motorcycle engines. The engines were loud and very close. *Too close.*

The three women began looking around the general area. They couldn't see anyone outside the fence line, instead the bikes came to them from the woods. They were far enough away from the clubhouse they couldn't get back before something happened.

On the other side of the fence line Whiskey, Micah and Lightning were astride their bikes. Slowly and carefully, Whiskey came up to the fence. Nudging it with his front tire, the complete eight foot section fell slowly to the ground, as if in slow motion.

The three women were stunned as the bikes moved over the chain link toward them in a matter of seconds.

Suddenly, the three bikes surrounded them, Whiskey pulled his knife and brandished it toward the women.

Micah grabbed Peaches.

Lightning grabbed Cassie's arm, pulling her toward him. Cassie screamed and struck out at him, catching him on the jaw.

Lightning let her go as his head snapped back. Growling, he grabbed at her again. This time he missed and Cassie's foot struck him in the thigh.

He howled as his bike tipped over, trapping him underneath the bulk of the vehicle. "You bitch!" He screamed. Pushing the bike off him, Lightning got to his feet and stomped over to where Cassie was standing. He tried to grab her again but now, Cassie was in fight mode and he didn't get close to her. She slipped from his grasp.

"Enough!" Whiskey yelled. "We don't have time for this shit." Pointing his knife at Melora, he told her. "I don't want these two but if you fight me here, one or both of them is gonna get hurt."

Melora glanced over at Peaches and Micah.

Micah had his arm around Peaches' throat with a gun pointed at her abdomen. Both she and Cassie stopped fighting. Lightning stepped in closer and smacked Cassie hard.

She went down to her knees and her mouth dripped blood. She glared up at the man standing beside her.

"Okay, Whiskey..." Melora gave up, raising her hands in surrender. "Let them go and I'll come with you without a fight. But if you hurt them in any way, I'll bring hell down on your head."

Whiskey smiled. "And just how do you plan to do that, baby girl? I'm the one with the power here, not you."

Melora sneered. "Only for the moment."

Whiskey laughed loudly as if what she said was truly hilarious. "Don't worry sweetheart, I'll make this quick. No one knows we're even here, so they won't find your body until we're long gone." His hand reached to his back and he brought out a gun. He cocked the weapon and pointed it at her. "We've been here too long. Get on behind Micah and don't give me any more problems. I won't hesitate to kill them if you do."

Melora hesitated then finally walked over to where Micah was parked.

Peaches stepped closer to Cassie and both women watched as Melora swung her leg over the bike.

Whiskey waved the weapon at the two women. "Because I got what I want, I'm letting you go. Don't make me regret it." He replaced the weapon and revved his engine. He waited while Lightning and Micah got on their bikes and then he turned and rode back into the woods.

The other two followed but Melora wasn't done yet. They were traveling quickly over rough terrain. Despite the bouncing, she noticed Micah and Lightning were having problems controlling their bikes. They almost took a header several times.

When Lightning came too close one time, Melora lifted her leg and kicked out at him.

Lightning lost control and ran into a tree.

Micah slowed down and eventually stopped. Turning his bike around he went back to where Lightning had crashed. Getting off, he went over to his friend and knelt down beside him. Micah could see his friend was dead. The unnatural angle of his neck and the bloody exposed wound on his scalp along with all the blood on his face and shoulders made him sick. He turned his head and glared at her.

Melora stared at the bike wrapped around the tree and blood on Lightning's face. She swallowed hard at the sight.

Micah stomped over to her and grabbed her wrists twisting them. He enjoyed the look of pain on her face. "You fucking bitch, try that again, and you'll be the one laying on the ground with blood all over your face. Whiskey isn't gonna like this!" He growled as he hauled her off his bike. When she was standing in front of him, Micah reached back with his fist and punched her hard in the belly.

Melora doubled over as she tried to gasp for breath. For a few minutes, she couldn't get the air inside her lungs and she could feel her head begin to swim due to the lack of oxygen. Then finally, she could breathe again.

Micah slapped her face not once but twice. Then he pushed her away from him and she fell to the ground. "Get up you sniveling little bitch! We have to find Whiskey and he isn't gonna be happy about your little stunt."

"Yeah, I'm real worried about what Whiskey's gonna like or not like," she gasped out as she got to her feet.

"You should be." Micah squeezed her wrist again. "He's gonna kill you real slow and enjoy it."

"Do you really think you'll even get the chance to leave this town?" She swung her leg over the bike and waited until Micah was mounted in front of her.

Micah started the bike and took off again through the wooded area. When they came out of the woods, the roar of the bike didn't seem so loud.

Melora leaned forward so the biker could hear her. "If you stay with Whiskey he's gonna get you killed."

Micah laughed out loud. "Nobody walks away from Whiskey. I don't have a choice anymore and neither do you. If you knew what was good for you, you wouldn't have let him catch up to you."

They headed into town, making their way through the side streets to the warehouse district.

Melora searched the shadows trying to find someone to help her but the darkness didn't reveal any of its secrets. She could only pray there was someone out there watching.

~ * * * * ~

When Cassie and Peaches burst through the back door of the clubhouse, Deke, Sam Raven, Gator and Mountain were just finishing their lunch. All of them got to their feet and rushed over to the women.

As Deke's arms went around her, Cassie peered up at him with tears in her eyes. "Whiskey took Melora," she whispered brokenly. Her hand grasped at his shirt and she repeated her statement. "The bastard took her and he's gonna kill her if we don't stop him!"

"How the hell did he get her?" Mountain shouted. "She was supposed to be protected behind the fence."

Izzy, Reva and some of the others came out of the kitchen at all the ruckus. They all stood in shock at the drama the women told them about.

Peaches shook her head. "Someone loosened part of the fence. Someone let that bastard in. He just pushed in a piece of the fence and it came down!"

Raven abruptly turned toward his men. All nine of them began looking at each other. Most eyes were trained on Gremlin.

He shook his head. "Fuck a duck, don't you guys have anything better to do than think I'm the traitor? Sweet baby Jesus...get a life."

Izzy gasped. "It was you..." She stared at the group of men standing there.

"What the fuck are you talking about?" Gremlin snarled.

"It was you all this time," she repeated her claim as she walked toward him.

"What are you saying?" Raven asked.

She turned to the leader of the Ghosts MC. "For two years, Whiskey forced me to work against my friend. I know you all think I betrayed her and I don't care about that. I always gave her that much time to escape but this one..." She turned to Gremlin. "This one has been plotting with Whiskey all along. I would wake up and overhear him on the phone with Jonesy and Whiskey all the time. I never knew who the traitor was until now."

"What makes you think it's Gremlin?" Raven asked.

"It's the way he said those two phrases together, fuck a duck and sweet baby Jesus. I've heard those phrases a lot in the past two years from the voice on the phone."

"She's lying!" Gremlin shouted. "She's nothing but a lying bitch just looking for a way to save her own ass."

Izzy moved closer and slapped him.

Gremlin raised his hand and was about to hit her back when Mountain moved in. He grabbed the other man's fist and squeezed.

Gremlin's face showed his pain as Mountain brought him to the floor with very little effort. "You're the real traitor here," Mountain grumbled. "You're the one who sold out his club for a worthless man. If Whiskey hurts my kid, I'm gonna take my time and kill him slowly, then I'm coming for you, you fucking coward. I'm going to peel your skin away one layer at a time until there's nothing left of you for the cops to identify." Mountain turned his head to glare at Raven. "Are you gonna stop me?"

Raven gave him a slow grin. "Nope. Although taking out the trash is club business I can overlook protocol this time."

Mountain turned back to Gremlin. "Now where the hell is Whiskey?"

Gremlin groaned from his position on the floor. Mountain was twisting his hand and the pain was becoming unbearable. "I don't know where he is!"

"Did you loosen the fence? Is that how he got in?" Raven asked.

"No, I swear it," Gremlin muttered in pain.

Izzy came over and began searching the man's pockets. Her hand clenched something and brought it out of the outer pocket of his vest. When she opened her hand, everyone could see the metal twisters that held the fence to the posts. She slowly turned her hand over and the half dozen metal links fell to the floor in front of Gremlin.

They hit the floor with a metallic clinking in the quiet of the room.

Mountain tightened his grip on the other man's closed fist. Gremlin shouted out his pain. "Where is he bastard?" Mountain demanded again.

"I don't know!" Gremlin growled between his clenched teeth.

"I know where he is." A voice from behind called out.

Everyone turned to see Zipper looking intently at his computer screen. When he glanced up at the room in general he said, "He's got her in the warehouse district. The old Butler building."

Mountain shoved Gremlin away and watched as the man slid on the floor in front of him. Looking up to where his men stood waiting he told them, "Tie this prick up and don't let him escape. I'll deal with him when I get back."

Chase and Rigger grabbed Gremlin and hauled him over to a vacant chair. Pushing the other man down, they were handed lengths of rope by some of the Sin's Bastards men. Tying him to the chair, they each took up positions on either side of the bound man.

"Who's coming with me?" Mountain asked the line of men behind him.

Sam and Raven took a step forward, as did Deke and Gator along with several of his own men. Mountain shook his head. "A smaller party would be better." He pointed to Sam and Raven. "If we take too many, he'll hear us and kill her before we can get to her." He stared at Deke. "Maybe you could send a wagon to bring the scum back for the tribunal. That way, he can be judged by his president and peers."

Deke nodded. Glancing over at some of his men, he motioned for them to do Mountain's bidding.

The rest of them watched as Mountain, Sam and Raven swiftly got ready to go. Each of them took out their choice of weapons and checked then replaced them. Finally, they began walking toward the door.

Before they could leave, Zipper came over and handed Sam a slip of paper. It held an address.

Sam nodded. He knew where the building was.

Izzy rushed forward and grabbed Mountain's arm. When he paused to look at her, she was crying. Tears rolled down her face as she begged him, "Please bring her back with you. I can't lose her now."

Without saying anything, he tore his arm away from her hold and continued toward the door.

No one said a word as they all watched the three men leave the building. The silence surrounding them was shattered as they heard three bikes start up and the grumble of the gate as it opened.

~****~

When Micah and Melora got to the warehouse and drove inside, she felt the cold of the building surrounding her. The place was cool and damp inside and the air inside smelled stale. They came to a stop well inside the building and the stark silence that surrounded them when they shut off the engines deafened her for a moment.

Whiskey looked around for Lightning. "What happened to Lightning?"

Micah nodded at Melora. "She ran him into a tree."

"Is he dead?"

Micah shrugged. "He wasn't looking too good the last I saw of him."

Whiskey growled. Getting off his bike, he reached out, grabbed her by the hair and hauled her off Micah's bike. "You bitch!" He growled. Turning, he dragged her by the hair to the steps and pulled her up three flights. He didn't care that he was pulling her hair out and Melora wouldn't give him the satisfaction of seeing her pain. He pushed her into one of the rooms along the hall to the left of the stairway.

Melora wanted to scream but she didn't. When he shoved her into the room, she saw the dirty quarters. At some point, someone had dragged a mattress into the room and left it behind. It was stained and filthy and there were several empty beer bottles on the floor. The one window in the room looked dirty and the glass was cracked but not broken. There were a couple of mismatched chairs in the room broken and stained with what looked like old blood.

There was a cooler in the corner of the room. The lid was broken and she could see and smell the dank liquid inside. Something floated in the dirty water but Melora didn't even want to know what it was. She shivered in dread.

Whiskey followed her into the room with a couple of lengths of rope in his hands. "Take your clothes off bitch." Whiskey growled as he paced in front of her.

"Why should I?"

"Mostly because I told you too, but also because I want to see the goods. I've been waiting for two years to get my hands on you and now I've got you."

"Go to hell."

Whiskey laughed. "I will after I send you there." He stepped closer. "Now take off your clothes."

"Fuck you," Melora grumbled. "But there's something you should know before you make any more stupid plans..." Melora taunted.

"What's that?" Whiskey sneered.

"Everyone who needs to know the truth about Baily does know what happened that night."

He shook his head. "They only know what you told them. It's your word against mine sweetheart. Walker would never believe your lies any more than Raven will."

Melora scoffed. "They know the truth. They saw the video I took that night."

Whiskey shrugged. "You mentioned a video before. How the hell did you take a video without anyone knowing?" He shook his head. "It doesn't matter. Videos can be doctored, it will still be your word against mine in the end."

"Yeah, except Raven was listening to you spout off about what you planned to do when you took over the club. He was right there when I made the phone call and he wasn't amused. Oh, and neither was Senator Walker. He thinks you're stupid if you think he would allow you to use his office to run guns and drugs. But now that he knows what happened to Baily, he's gonna have everyone out there looking for you. Not only the cops but Raven's men will be looking too. You may not care about the Ghosts but you have no clue who those women you assaulted belonged to. There are three clubs here, Sin's Bastards brought together not only Satan's Spawn but Boston's Sinners and Bangor's Satan's Bastards. Oh and then there's my dad. He's president of the Sons of Satan, all the way from Texas. If you hurt me, you won't be safe anywhere. But hell, that don't matter now, I guess. They're all gonna hunt you down and not even worry about burying your bodies. They will leave you for the rats."

Micah groaned. "Shit!"

Whiskey's face paled but he recovered quickly. "So? Raven was bound to find out sooner or later. All I have to do is step up the timeline. As far as the rest goes, well they have to find me first." He shrugged. "I know all about the Sons of Satan, our club has dealt with them in the past. I'm not worried about them."

Melora sneered. "You should be. Raven's not going to protect you or your crew this time. Not like he did when you shot that guy in the back when he was alone in the dark. You can always duck and run like the bitch you really are."

Whiskey glared at her as his hands shook, but didn't bother answering her challenge. He walked to her and raising his hand, he hit her hard. When she stumbled and fell to the floor, he grabbed her by her shirt and ripped it from her body. She jerked as he pulled the material away from her torso. He tossed the shirt and the denim vest into the corner of the room.

Grabbing both her wrists, he dragged her over to one of the chairs. Pushing her down into the seat, he tied one wrist to the arm of the chair with a length of rope. With the other length of rope, he tied her other wrist to the opposite arm.

The bindings were so tight, she couldn't move and her fingers began to tingle as the circulation was cut off to her hands.

Whiskey's hands went to the zipper on her pants and he ripped it down. Grabbing the waistband of her jeans, he tore them down her legs, nearly pulling her from the chair. He left her in her underwear and began to pace back and forth in front of her.

Micah joined them and stared at the girl.

Melora could see lust in his eyes.

"So now what, boss?" he asked. "What the hell are we gonna do now?"

"Shut up." Whiskey shouted at him. "I need to think."

"Yeah, well think fast okay?" Micah urged. "If what she says is true, it won't take them long to find us and I want to be long gone when they get here."

Whiskey stopped and stared at the other man. "So what? They find us, or they'll find her barely alive and we'll be long gone. They don't know where we are."

"We gotta get out of town while we can." Micah grabbed his arm. "We don't have time to take her out!"

Whiskey wrenched his arm away from Micah's hold. "We got time to make her suffer. Yes, they might know we're here but they don't know where here is. Now settle down and let me do my thing." He stared at Melora and licked his lips. "I've been waiting two years for this and I will not be denied." Whiskey reached behind his back and grabbed the handle of his knife from the sheath inside the back of his vest. Pulling it around to his front, he twisted the handle in his hands. "This is gonna be fun." His eyes glazed over and for a moment, he was lost in thoughts of pain-pleasure he knew was coming.

Melora's heart pounded in her chest. Her skin crawled just having these two men this close to her. She knew the look in Whiskey's eyes. She'd seen it before, the last time was the night Baily died. She knew how Whiskey got so tied up in what he could do with that damn knife of his and she knew he was one who enjoyed bringing others pain. She just never thought he would catch her and now she was afraid he would bring her world to a nasty ending. She almost prayed for death to find her quickly.

Her eyes focused on the vest Zipper had given her yesterday. She prayed the tracking device he told her was working. All she had to do was wait and pray the guys got here in time. She really wanted the chance to finally know her father and to find a future with Sam. In that moment, she realized something. She loved that old man. She loved him with everything she had and she desperately wanted a future with him beyond the here and now.

Glancing up at Whiskey and Micah, she knew her future was very limited. She also knew Whiskey was going to take his sweet time in delivering her to the hands of Hades.

Chapter Twelve

Whiskey paused in front of her chair and stared at her for a moment. His cold gaze traveled up and down her body while his eyes dulled with lust. He twisted the knife in his hand and he checked out her body carefully. He watched as her breasts moved up and down with each trembling breath she took. Her breasts were full and almost bursting out of her bra. He licked his lips as he watched her face. Finally, he saw the fear she was trying so hard not to let out. Her fear wasn't strong enough yet to give him the high he so eagerly sought, but he knew he could get it there.

Whiskey licked his lips again as the fear in her eyes grew. He lifted the knife and laid the blade on her skin just above her belly button. He drew a line across her belly. The blade touching her just hard enough to break the skin but not enough to really make her bleed. "Did you know one of the eastern continents, I'm not sure if it's Japan or China or somewhere in between, has this torture called the death of a thousand cuts?" he asked her softly. "It doesn't really matter where it came from I guess, only that it's out there somewhere."

Melora held still as he stood closer.

Again, he lifted the knife and cut her, not very deep but enough to get the blood flowing. This time, the knife wrapped around her side. He lifted the knife to her chest. "Did you also know you can stab the body in several places and not kill a person? That if you do it the right way, you can deliver however many stab wounds you want and the person will never die, at least not from being stabbed, she will die from blood loss first, well that's the theory anyway. I've never tried it before now. When I stab someone, I want to do the most damage I can but I guess you know that don't you?"

The cuts on her belly hadn't actually hurt, they only caused her discomfort. Taking a deep breath and praying the knife wouldn't slip, Melora answered him, "Yeah, I've seen your handiwork."

Whiskey smiled. "That's right you have, you were there the night Baily died. You saw what I did to him."

Melora sneered. "You are one sick puppy, you know that?"

Whiskey shrugged. "The little sniveling bitch thought he could bargain with me. I'm not the one who borrowed money from the club. I'm not the one who thought he could get out of paying it back or thought he could use his uncle as a bargaining chip. I'm just the one who taught the boy some manners."

"You murdered him!" Melora all but shouted. "How the hell was Raven supposed to collect his money from a dead man?"

Again, Whiskey shrugged. "At the time, I didn't care one way or the other. It wasn't my money and his debt carried over to other members of the brat's family. His mother paid it back and that's all Raven was looking for. She thought paying off the debt would get her the location of his body or at least that's what she was told. Although, the debt would have been settled anyway by the Senator. Too bad, she'll never know exactly what happened to him."

"Sure she will," Melora interjected.

Whiskey grinned. "And how will that happen? The hogs took care of his body. There wasn't anything left of Baily to worry about."

"That's where you would be wrong, you psycho bastard" she assured him.

"What do you mean by that?" Micah spoke up.

She turned toward the other man. "It means...*asshole*, if anything happens to me Baily's body will show up along with a copy of the video I took that night. Everyone and his brother will know what really happened and who did it."

"That's not possible." Whiskey paled.

"Oh, it's more than possible," Melora stated in a firm voice.

Whiskey stared at her for the longest time then shrugged. "I don't believe it. You couldn't have known where we put him that night. We weren't followed and the hogs would have been called by the scent of his blood." He moved the knife to the top of her chest just below her collarbone. He angled the tip of the knife away from her skin "Here for instance...is a very good place to sink a knife into a body. If you do it right, there are no major blood vessels or organs to hit. " He suggested as he slid the knife through her skin. The blade went through her muscle and struck bone on the other side.

Melora felt faint as the blade pierced her body. She felt like screaming but couldn't get any sound out of her throat.

He didn't extract the blade right away and when he did, he twisted it slightly, doing the maximum amount of damage with the minimum amount of effort. Blood flowed freely from the wound, washing down her chest to pool at her waist.

Whiskey moved a step or two away, then studied her for a moment. When he returned to her this time, he placed the blade against her right side. Pushing the blade into her body he told her, "Here is another good place. It hurts like a sonofabitch but doesn't really do that much damage."

Melora began to sweat as she tried hard not to cry out her pain. When she felt him twist the knife, she moaned but didn't scream. When he pulled the knife from her body, she felt the gush of blood run down her side and pool underneath her. She raised her head to glare at him.

~****~

Whiskey smiled. He could feel his body respond to the pain and fear in her eyes even if she wasn't screaming yet, he knew she soon would be. Then and only then, would he feel complete. Only then would his taste for pain and torture be complete. His body began to crave the end that would only come when she acknowledged the pain.

He was about to find a third nonlethal spot when the door to the room they were in flew open and several men rushed inside. He felt the sudden pain explode inside his head as a huge fist hit him in the face. He dropped to his knees in stunned disbelief.

Then he felt something hard hit the back of his neck and everything went dark. The knife tumbled from his blood soaked hand.

~****~

Mountain glanced over at Raven as he saw the other man uppercut Micah.

Micah flew backwards hitting the wall hard. He slid down the wall and lay there crumpled on the floor.

Mountain turned to the other side and watched as Sam grabbed Whiskey's knife off the floor and cut the ropes holding Melora to the chair. He knelt beside her and grabbed one of her hands rubbing her wrist as his eyes traveled over her bruised and bloody body. "Are you okay baby?" he whispered.

Melora turned her head and saw the concern in his eyes. "It's nothing that time won't heal," she whispered.

Sam removed his own shirt and draped it over her abused body. "Deke is coming with a vehicle. We'll get you to the hospital, so they can patch you up."

Melora shook her head. "No hospital. They'll ask too many questions." She tried to explain in a breathless voice. "Can't someone at the clubhouse take care of this?"

"Maybe she's right," Raven suggested. "We can't exactly bring the police into this."

Sam lifted her into his arms. "Raine can take care of her. He's dealt with worse than this."

Melora lifted her arms to circle Sam's neck. Laying her head on his shoulders she asked, "What's going to happen to Whiskey and Micah?"

"Where is the third guy, Lightning?" Raven asked.

Melora's lips curled upward. "He's in the woods wrapped around a tree."

Raven's brows went up. "How the hell did that happen?"

She shrugged. "There might have been some speed, rough terrain and a helping kick involved in there somewhere."

Raven snorted, looking at Mountain and Sam. "We'll have to look for him in a day or two. Might not be safe out there at the moment, with all the wolves in the area."

"At least he ain't feeding the wild hogs," Mountain sneered.

"Guys, I hate to rush this conversation but she's still bleeding here," Sam called out in a worried voice as he walked back to the door. Before he could go through it however, Deke, Gator and several other guys from the club rushed in.

Deke told the others to bind Whiskey and Micah. "Tie them up and throw them in the back of the truck. One of you guys will have to bring Sam's bike back to the clubhouse too."

"And mine," Mountain told them. "I'm riding back with my daughter."

Melora lifted one hand from Sam's shoulder and reached out for her father.

Mountain took her hand in his and held it close to his heart. Then lifted it to his lips and kissed her fingers softly.

Then she turned back into Sam's shoulder and groaned.

Mountain looked around the room and saw her clothing. Picking it up, he followed Sam and found them sitting in a truck just inside the building.

Sam was sitting in the back seat of the truck with Melora on his lap.

Mountain leaned over them and lifted Sam's shirt out of the way. Pulling her away from Sam slightly, he balled Melora's shirt up and pressed it against the bleeding wound on her chest.

Melora groaned but didn't fight him. The bleeding had almost stopped and the pressure from his hand would stop it altogether. Next, he grabbed a towel from the seat next to where they were sitting. Moving down to her other stab wound, he pressed the towel against that wound. Then he pressed her against Sam again, and nodded. "That should hold until we get back to the clubhouse." He turned to glare at Sam. "I hope your man can deal with this. She's lost a lot of blood."

Sam nodded and held her close. "Raine can deal with this," he assured the other man. "Can you?"

Mountain glared at Sam. "Yeah, I can deal." He backed up and slammed the back door shut, then climbed into the front passenger seat slamming that door shut as well.

Then they all waited for the others to put Whiskey and Micah's bodies into the back. Deke got into the driver's seat and without a word, drove out of the warehouse and back to the compound.

~****~

Melora curled up in Sam's arms, glad the nightmare was over. Lifting her lips to his neck she whispered, "Thank you for coming for me, Bones." Her lips pressed a kiss to his neck.

His arms tightened around her and he softly kissed the top of her head. "I think you knew I would come for you, Silk," he whispered back. "I'd have to be dead not to come after you."

Melora tightened her grip on him without saying a word. Closing her eyes, she rested for a moment then Deke hit a pothole and jarred her. She hissed then groaned in pain.

"Hush now darlin," Sam whispered. "It will be okay. I promise."

"As long as I'm with you I'll be fine. Just don't let me go."

"I won't," Sam vowed.

Melora sighed and closed her eyes, knowing Sam would keep her safe.

~****~

An hour later, Raine put the last bandage in place and began cleaning up around him.

Melora had her wounds tended to under the watchful eyes of her father and Sam.

Raine had draped a towel over her girly parts while he tended her wounds, so neither man would feel the need to beat the hell out of him. He looked over at the girl and caught her smile. He grinned as he lifted a t-shirt off a pile of towels and helped her into it. As she tugged the garment down, he pulled the towel out from underneath and lifted the blanket to cover her bottom half. "That should do it," he finally told her. "I'll keep an eye on things for the next day or so, but you should be okay."

"What about all the blood she lost?" Mountain asked with concern all over his face.

"Her own body can replace that if she rests," Raine assured them. "Then we need to get plenty of fluids and food into her. I'll have Reva bring her something hot and filling in a little while but for now, I think she should sleep." He got to his feet and stared at the two other men in the room. "I've given her something for the pain and she needs the rest. Don't you guys have some business to take care of?"

Mountain pushed himself away from the wall. "Yeah, we do." He tapped Sam on the shoulder and turned to leave the room.

Before he could get too far, Melora called him back, "Daddy?"

Mountain halted in his tracks, his face paling at the endearment he thought he would never hear. He slowly turned then stepped over to the bed.

She reached out and grabbed his hand.

Mountain gently squeezed her fingers. Looking at her, he could see the struggle she was going through. He leaned over her and gently pressed his lips to her forehead. "I'll be here if you want to talk later."

She smiled softly. "I'd like that. I'd like that very much."

Mountain kissed her cheek then stood up tall and straight. He nodded at Sam then left the bedroom.

Sam went over to the bed and leaned down to kiss her forehead. "I'll be back." He straightened up and turned to leave.

Melora reached out and grabbed his hand.

Sam turned to look at her his hand reaching up to smooth her silky hair away from her face.

"Make him suffer," she whispered. "He's caused too much pain and agony in this world. Give him some of it back."

Sam smiled slightly. "I don't think that will be a problem. This time, it's a matter of more than just bones, baby girl. If I can't break him, Mountain will."

After he was gone, Raine caught her glance. "That man loves you."

Melora smiled. "I know. I love him too." She chuckled. "I never thought I would ever say that about someone."

"Why?" Raine asked. "You're young enough to fall in love several times over."

She shook her head. "My mother only ever loved one man. That man just walked out of this room. She never loved anyone the way she loved him and when he left her behind, she never forgot him either. She taught me about that kind of love and I've never felt it until the day I met Sam. It was so strong and so sudden, I never knew what hit me. I never thought about it until then. Now, I can't imagine my life without him in it. I don't think I even want to try." Melora closed her eyes and drifted to sleep.

Raine felt surprised at this news. He'd known Bones for a very long time and suddenly, he saw him through this girl's eyes and he shook his head. "I'll be Goddamned." Then he stood for a long moment just staring at her. Finally, he raised the blanket up and over her then turned to leave.

~****~

Whiskey shook his head and tried to clear away the fog. He registered the pain pounding in his head but couldn't remember where it came from. His whole body hurt and he didn't know why. He struggled to open his eyes but couldn't quite manage it. He must have had a hell of a party last night.

A few minutes later, he came to again. This time, his head began to clear. He heard men talking in the background but couldn't make out what they were saying. Shaking his head, he felt the pain but it was clearer now, sharper even than it had been before.

He lifted his head and opened his eyes. Glancing around, he noted they were in the woods. They were in a clearing surrounded by trees. He tried to move but found he couldn't. Lifting his head, he saw he was bound to a pole. His hands were pulled above his head and tied. He also found he'd and the others had been stripped of their clothing. All they had left on their bodies were underwear. Their vests were laying in the dirt in front of them with all the patches removed and shredded.

Turning his head, he saw Micah and Gremlin were also bound and tied to poles. Both men were sweating but silent as they awaited what was coming next.

Finally, the others noticed he was awake and Whiskey watched as several men came to stand in front of him. He knew Raven but he didn't know the others. "What the fuck is going on here?" he demanded.

"This is a tribunal," Raven informed him. "MC laws demand a tribunal judgment when treason is charged against a member."

Whiskey sneered. "What charge of treason?"

"You and the others have been charged with treason against the Ghosts of Dixie, The Sin's Bastards, and the Sons of Satan MC."

"What the fuck did I ever do to the Sin's Bastard and the Sons of Satan MC?" Whiskey demanded.

"You took my woman," Sam replied.

"You shot my man in the back, paralyzing him for life, then you kidnapped my daughter," Mountain spoke next.

Whiskey snorted. "I don't know your woman, old man and I sure as hell don't know your daughter." He ignored the other charge completely. If they had the proof it was him they would have done something about it by now.

Mountain smiled. "Sure you do, Whiskey. She's the one you were giving lessons to about all the ways you could stab a person without killing them."

Whiskey paled. "Melora Shaw is your daughter?"

Beside him, Micah groaned in disgust. "Fuck! She was telling the truth."

Sweat beaded Whiskey's forehead but he tried to bluff his way through it.

"Yeah, how is that for a kick in the head?" Mountain grinned. He turned his head to glare at Micah who for some reason couldn't or wouldn't meet his eyes.

Sam stepped forward and raised his hand to Whiskey. In his hand was Whiskey's blade. It was still covered in Melora's blood. Without losing eye contact with the other man, Sam simply shoved the blade into Whiskey's shoulder. The action wasn't slow or gentle like Whiskey's had been—no, Sam's thrust was more brutal. It was the same place Whiskey had stabbed Melora.

Whiskey drew in a deep breath but didn't say anything. When Sam twisted the knife around and pulled the blade out Whiskey smiled. "You're gonna have to do better than that old man."

Sam's smile deepened and he moved the blade to Whiskey's side. Slipping the knife in deep, he twisted the blade a bit then pulled it out again.

Whiskey groaned but otherwise remained silent.

Then Sam raised the blade to his other shoulder and dug the blade in deeper.

Blood ran freely down his body. Whiskey felt the pain of his wounds but he'd felt this pain before and it didn't seem to faze him that much.

Just then, Sam noticed the old scars. They covered most of his chest and arms. Cut scars, some looked old while others were barely healed. All of the old scars looked to be self-inflicted. He shook his head. "You don't even feel the pain anymore do you...you crazy fuck?"

Whiskey smiled. "Oh, I still feel it, I just don't let it rule me like it once did."

"Maybe you won't feel it in the non-lethal places, nutjob," Sam countered. "But you might feel it where it hurts more." He pulled the huge bloody knife back again.

"No wait!" Raven called out. Stepping up to Mountain and Sam, he raised his hand to stop them. "We have to do this according to the MC laws."

"And they are?" Mountain asked.

"With everyone present, we read the charges and take a vote."

All three men looked around at the number of men standing beside them.

Raven's men were all there, as were Mountain's men. Deke's men were also present. Sam's men stood around the edge of the group too. They turned and saw Iceman leaning against a tree on the outer edge of the clearing. Beside him stood his men.

When Iceman noticed them looking at him he pushed away from the tree and came over to join the others. He met their gazes straight up then turned to the three men bound to the poles. "Which one of these bastards held a gun to my wife's head?" Iceman asked quietly.

Anyone who knew him would have known that tone in his voice. Iceman was not a man others took for a fool. When his voice reached the tone it was at now—that's when he was at his most dangerous.

Everyone looked at the three men and it was Micah they all stared at.

Iceman walked up to the other man and spoke softly, "I guess that would be you, huh?"

"I was just following orders." Micah trembled.

Iceman turned to gaze at Whiskey for a moment then turned back to Micah. "And were you and your other friend just following orders when he hit Cassie, not once but several times? And what about after the fact when Melora made him run into a tree? Were you just following orders when you dragged her off your bike and beat the hell out of her in the woods?"

Micah paled and began to shake. Each word striking him as if Iceman was using his fists.

"Your friend, the one they called Lightning, he deserved to die for what he did to Cassie. Melora got justice for her but I'm gonna get justice for Peaches. Sam over there, is gonna get justice for his woman." He leaned closer to Micah.

Micah was so scared the sweat rolled off his face.

"You see, I made my woman a vow that nobody would *ever* hurt her again. Nobody would ever scare her that way again either and...you did both shithead." Iceman took a step away and watched along with the others as Micah wet himself. Sneering, he shook his head. Turning his head to Raven he said, "Call out the charges and then call for the vote. But before everyone votes, maybe it's time they see what Whiskey did to Baily and maybe they should hear what his plans for the club were gonna be. I don't think everyone here knows what he had planned."

Raven nodded. "That sounds fair enough."

Melora's video was passed from man to man, even those who weren't Ghosts.

Whiskey could almost feel the crowds' displeasure growing and for the first time, he began to feel the pain of betrayal. He began to feel the nerve endings all over his body tingling and the hairs on the back of his head began to itch.

The charges against them were read and the crowd immediately called out their guilty vote.

Raven motioned for two of his men to carry out the sentence of death but Deke stopped him.

Everyone turned to stare at him for a moment.

Deke shrugged. "While I totally agree with the findings of the tribunal, I think poetic justice should be administered here."

"What kind of poetic justice?" Raven asked. "What do you have in mind?"

"Exactly what they wanted for Baily," Deke told the group. "We feed them to the hogs."

"Do you have wild hogs up here?" Raven asked.

Deke grinned. "No but we have a neighbor who has several sows that will eat anything put in front of them. He also has a couple of mean sows. They really tear into their food and devour it quickly, so there's never a trace."

"I like your idea." Mountain nodded.

Sam stepped forward and made a brushing motion toward Micah and Gremlin. "Those two deserve death before consumption but I think Whiskey deserves to feel everything he has coming."

"I like that idea even better." Mountain gave him a cold grin.

Whiskey stared at them without seeing them. He was trying to escape to the place in his mind that would help him block out all the pain but it wasn't working. He could still hear everything going on around him. When he heard the two shots that echoed in the woods, he was startled enough to look beside him. He saw Micah and Gremlin hanging limp against the poles and he knew for them, the nightmare was over.

Several men gathered around him and one began tying his feet together while another one cut the rope holding him in place. His hands were still bound but when they pulled him away from the pole, Whiskey began to fight in earnest.

It didn't take much to subdue him and as they carried him away he began to beg and plead for his life.

The group as a whole marched behind him in stony silence and a few minutes later, they paused and waited to watch as the small group made their way to the fence line beyond.

The air here was stagnate with the scent of pigs and garbage. Whiskey felt his body being lifted up and dumped over the fence line. He landed with a hard thump into the mud. The sounds and scents came right up into Whiskey's face and he let out an inhuman scream as a hog's face came right up close to him and opened its drooling jaws.

~* * *~

Raven, Mountain, Sam, Iceman and Deke along with the others watched from the other side of the fence. When the hogs noticed them, they all came running over and then the sounds of grunting hogs and Whiskey's screams was all that could be heard.

When the sounds finally died down, none of the men smiled, they all did what had to be done. In silence everyone turned and headed back the way they came.

~* * *~

It took three days of complete bed rest before Melora felt good enough to even sit up in bed. By the end of the third day, she was going stir crazy. Pushing the blankets aside, she swung her legs over the edge of the bed and stood up. She felt dizzy for a moment but as soon as her head cleared, she made her way slowly to the dresser. Opening a drawer, she pulled out one of Sam's t-shirts and a pair of sweatpants. She had to roll the pants up several times before she could even take a step without tripping but finally, she was ready to go.

Brushing her long hair back away from her face, she made her way to the door. She had to stand there for a moment to gather her strength.

Just moving a little bit left her trembling but she knew if she gave in to the weakness, she probably wouldn't go anywhere for a while.

She opened the door and gradually made her way down the hall and into the great room.

Everyone sitting there stopped talking the moment she showed herself.

She could see them all, Mountain, Sam, Deke and Cassie, Iceman, Peaches and Raven. They were sitting at the main table in the room. The only one missing was Izzy.

Melora straightened her shoulders and carefully made her way over to them. She didn't ask for their help nor would she have accepted it and they all knew it. It was the longest walk of her life but she made it.

Sam stood and brought her to him. When he sat down, his arms cradled her to his lap. "Are you okay?" he whispered in her ear.

Melora nodded and looked at everyone. Shrugging, she put off their concerns. "I was bored in that bedroom all by myself."

Raven smiled. "I'm leaving in the morning and I hoped I would get the chance to say goodbye."

Melora reached out her hand and when he took it she asked, "Are we good?"

Raven nodded. "Yeah, we're good. Whiskey's threat is over and I'm going home to pick up the pieces and try to get things back on the right track."

"Before you go, I need to give you something."

"What would that be?" Raven looked curious.

"The location of Baily's body. I told the Senator when this was over, I would release his body for the family to get closure. I think they deserve that much, don't you?"

Raven nodded. "Yeah, they do. I appreciate it and I know they will as well."

"It was the right thing to do. I couldn't let Whiskey win this one and Baily might have been a dumbass, but he didn't deserve to die like that. Nobody does."

"For the record, I never told Whiskey to jump him that night," Raven assured her. "I know now that it was Whiskey who lent him the money and Whiskey was the one blackmailing him to get him in a position he could use to get the Senator under his thumb. That's not the way my club is supposed to work." Raven shrugged. "Would I love a political connection? Who wouldn't? Am I going to use blackmail and the threat of violence to get it...No way. That always comes back to bite you in the ass in the end. Some of the boys and I have been talking about coming clean. We may be a motorcycle club and all but who says we can't be legit? I've been watching things around here and so far, I like what I see and what's more, I don't think I'll have too much trouble selling it to the rest of them." He shook his head. "Hell, I'm getting too old for most of the horseshit anyway."

"Maybe returning Baily to his family will help smooth things over then," Melora offered.

Raven grinned. "I can say it's been a pleasure to finally meet you, Miss Melora Shaw."

"Maybe the next time I'm in Raleigh, I'll look you up." Melora nodded. "Maybe."

Before she could do anything else, the backdoor opened and Izzy walked in holding one of Cassie's babies. She glanced up and saw Melora. Yelping, she rushed over to the table. Handing the baby to her mother, she went over to Melora and hugged her tight. "Damn girl, don't ever do that again." Izzy gave her grief. "I never thought I'd see you again."

Melora smiled. "You should know better by now. How many times have we been in trouble together? Don't I always come back from it?"

Izzy chuckled. "More times than I care to remember, that's for sure but this time was different and you know it. This time, you might not have come back. I was really afraid for you."

Melora raised her hand and cupped it around Izzy's cheek. "I wouldn't do that to you. We've been through too much together to start thinking like that."

Izzy began to cry. She fell to her knees and wrapped her arms around Melora's waist. "This time, you weren't alone with just me looking out for you."

Mountain couldn't stand to listen to the heartbreak in Izzy's voice anymore. He scooped her up off the floor and held her on his lap. "This time, neither of you are alone. As long as you are part of Melora's family, you're part of mine too."

Izzy wrapped her arms around the big guys' neck. Glancing over at her friend, she tipped her head at Mountain. "So this Mountain man is your daddy?"

"Yup, sure is." Melora grinned.

"And that's your old man?" She nodded at Bones.

"Yup, sure is," Sam answered for her, his arms tightening around Melora's waist.

"I can deal with that." Izzy smiled.

Next up

Karma's Bite
Book Two
Sin's Bastards Mc Series

About K. J. Dahlen

K.J. Dahlen

Author of the bestselling award winning Bratva Brothers and Satan Spawns MC Series...

I live in a small town (population 1,000) in Wisconsin. From my deck, I can see the Mississippi River on one side and the bluffs, where eagles live and nest on the other side. I live with my husband Dave and dog Bella. My two children are grown and I have two grandchildren and two great-grands.

I love to watch people and that has helped me with my writing. I often use people I watch as characters in my books and I always try to give my characters some of my own values and habits.

I love to create characters and put them in a troubling situation then sit back and let them do all the work. My characters surprise even me at times. At some point in the book, they take on a life of their own and the twists and turns they create becomes the story. Of all the stories, I could write I found I like mystery/thrillers the best. I like to keep my readers guessing until the very end of the book.

Join K.J. Dahlen's Reader Group[1]
Newsletter[2]

1. https://www.facebook.com/groups/1538834079503734/

2. https://confirmsubscription.com/h/j/C38BC78874901A2F

Also by Kj Dahlen

Badass Women
Badass Women-Savaged Sous MC
Badass Women-Sin's Bastards
Badass Women#3 Brothers Of Chaos
Badass Women-Bratva Blood Brothers
Badass Women-Lost Sons MC
Badass Women VIM
Badass Women-Bratva New York

Bikers Of The Rio Grande
Rambler
Hunter
Sinner
Bearcat
Wizard
Raven
Taz
Thunder
Thunder & A Little Bit Of Lightning
Snowman & Eden

Born Of Desperation
Nitro
Pagan
Repo
Typhoon
Montana
Capone
Dixon

Bratva Blood Brothers
Yuri
Mikial
Barshan
Sazon
Roman
Brothers United
losif
Kosta
Nikoli
Nicky
Sergi
Misha
Timor
Felix
Kirill
Sasha
Maxim, A Bratva Christmas
A Bratva Christmas
Mikial-Father's Day

Valentines-Bratva
Sergi's Father's Day
Bratva Blood Brothers Thanksgiving

Bratva Born
Nubric
Koyla
Petrov
Minki
Dima
Catch
Bratva Women-Prequel-Bratva Born

Bratva Enforcers-Nomads
Viktor
Ivan
Adrik
Andrey
Grisha
Matvey

Bratva New Orleans
Bratva New Orleans#1
Bratva New Orleans#2
Bratva New Orleans
Bratva New Orleans#4

Bratva New York
Nikoli Bratva New York
Misha-New York
Nicky-New York
Felix-New York
Kirill Bratva New York
Sergi Bratva New York
Bratva New York
Christmas-Bratva New York
Crimson- Special Edition

Brothers At Arms MC
Zeus
Diabolus
Memphis
Grave Digger
Click
Captain

Cajun Kings
Cajun King
Fat Tuesday
Born In Fahyuh
Crazy As Hell
Sweet Rascal
I Don't Give A Damn

Cajun Queens

Cajun Queens

Cajun Queens#2

Cajun Queens #3

Cajun Queens #4

Cajun Queens #5

Cajun Queens#6

Crimson Tide MC

Tracker

Boomer

Cyrus

Clovis

Vance

Tether

Crimson Tide MC

Destiny Meets Fate

Destiny Meets Fate

Destiny Meets Fate#2

Destiny Meets Fate#3

Destiny Meets Fate

Destiny Meets Fate

Destiny Meets Fate #6

Destiny Meets Fate Set

Devil's Advocates MC
Jackal
Beast
Wolf
Apollo
Shade
Tank
Shadow Hunter
Devil's Advocates Series Set

Devil's Own MC
Stormy

Devils Trifecta MC
Gage
Joker
Sledge
Devil's Trifecta MC Set

Fire And Ice
Fire And Ice
The Flame
Invincible
Supernatural
Incandescent
Extraordinary

Ghost Riders MC
Pepper
Phantom
Dax
Venom
Heathen
NiteStalker

Hell's Bloodhounds MC
Barron
Leonid

Hell's Fire Riders
A Hell's Fire Christmas

Hell's Fire Riders MC
Pappy's Shadow
Betrayed
Trigger The Storm
Shay
Legend
Birth Of Hells Fire Rider
Trudy

Kings Of Wrath MC
Pride
Candyman
Rage
Scar
Romeo
Cosmos
Kings Of Wrath
Kings Of Wrath Christmas

Lords Of Hell MC
Mayhem
Brutus
Bear
Stone
Tag
Svante

Lost Sons MC
Creed's Return
Jack
Tate
Harry
Silas
Daniel
Silas & Midge
Come Home-Lost Sons MC
Lost Sons MC

Louisiana Heat
Ajax
Fireball
Stinger
Moon
Racer
Player
LA Heat Series

Malverde
Malverde
Malverde 2
Malverde 3

Masters Of Mayhem MC
Rance
Bull
Korbel
Rocker
Nova
Ram

Misfits Of Whiskey Bend
Misfits Of Whiskey Bend

New Blood-Savaged Souls MC
Arrow
Beau
Hayes
Runner
Acer
Duke
New Blood Savaged Souls-Boxed Set

Payback
Ghoster

Phantom Fury MC
Shilo
Bullet

Princes Of Hell MC
Talon
Rogue
Falcon
Condor
Princes Of Hell MC Set

Reunion Series

Reunion
Silk & Bones Reunion
Hell's Fire Riders Reunion
Yuri Bratva Blood Brothers Reunion
Rogue's Of Hell MC-Reunion
Reunion Sin's Bastards MC- Next Generation

Rivers Foundation
Cade

Rogues Of Hell MC
Titan
Kota
Brute
Nash
Wanderer
Hawkins
Rogues Of Hell MC Set
Rogues Christmas

Rogues Of Hell MC Trilogy
Cash

Rogues Trilogy
Wilder

San Francisco Steel
Slammer
Shotgun
Grinder
Mammoth
Booker
Spider
Texas

Satan's Spawn MC
Spawn & Spitfire
Revenge and Retribution
Babies & Bastards

Savaged Souls MC
Boone
Gunner
Jett
Cobra
Thor
Gypsy
Grizzly
Moose
Skeeter

Shades of Shay Trilogy

Shades Of Shay
Shades Of Shay
Shades Of Shay

Shadow Warriors
Blue

Silver Warriors
The Quest
The Ride
The Brothers
The Game
The Fall
The Race
Coming Home
Silver Warriors-Boxed Set
Silver Warriors Halloween

Sinners MC
Hawk
Pony
Prosper
Saber
Rebel
Buzz
Sinners- Boxed Set

Sinners Of Boston
V-Sins & Sinners
Atlas
Echo
Cuffs
Ringo
Dak

Sin's Bastards MC
Silk & Bones
Karma's Bite
No Regrets
Hell's Fury
Lies & Liars
Stone Cold
Sin's Bastards Christmas
Leon
Mountain
Peaches & Iceman
Girl's Night
Sin's Bastards Mother's Day
Bane Returns
Christmas With The Sin's
Deacon
Reva

Sin's Bastards Next Generation
Raine

Chance
Gambler
Bowie
Judge
Byron
Hound
Dante
Iceman
The Kids
Wiley
Calderone
Sin's Bastards MC Next Generation Boxed Set #1
Vincinti Women
Sin's Bastards Next Generation Boxed Set #2
Jericho's Christmas

Soldiers Of Hades MC
Cottonmouth
Python
GTO
Lightning
Whiskey
Spirit
Cobra's New Year
Soldiers Of Hades Christmas

Sons Of Ireland
Sons of Ireland-Boston#1
Sons Of Ireland

Stone Cold Bitches MC
Calypso
Widowmaker
Aqua Velvet
Medusa
Razor
Ruby Red
Stone Cold Bitches MC Set

Swamp Patriots
Swamp Patriots

Tennessee Breeds
Breed
Greer
Monster
Crow
Maverick
Cowboy
Blade
Tennessee Breeds Set

The Boondocks
Mad Dog
Stroker

Vengeance Is Mine
Bane
Damon
Bane's Shadow
Cane
The Priest
Kill Me Twice
Kill Me Again
Lionheart
Lancelot
Galahad
PenDragon
Excaliber
Palamedes
Calegis
Escalades
Theo
Hell's Vengeance
Archangel
Butterfly
Blue Eyes
Dante's Inferno
Conquest
Apocalypse
Poison
Into The Black
White Noise
Absolute
Doom
Faith
VIM Set

Bane's Infinity
Valiant
VIM #2

VIM Redux
VIM Redux

Vincintis
The Vincintis
The Vincintis#2
The Vincintis#3
The Vincintis#4

WarLords MC
Truman
King
Jack- WarLords
Deuce
Joker
Traven
Giving Thanks-Warlord MC

Whiskey Bend MC Series
Lucifer's Woman
Demon's Stand
At All Costs

Out Of The Shadows
Jinx
Shadow
Cooper
Bender
Saint
Whiskey Bend MC Set
Christmas In Whiskey Bend
Whiskey Bend Easter
Misfits Christmas

Wings Of Fire MC
Maze
Tabor
Sayer
Hellion

Standalone
Hell's Fire MC Series Set
Satan's Spawn & Sin's Bastards Collection
A Life For Luke
Chasing Eve
Saving Sebastian
Shadows Of The Past
Never Forget Me
The Cartouche
A Wrath Is Born
The New Brotherhood
Slade
Zipper

Carson
San Francisco Steel MC Set
Return To Yuri
Patriot
Badass Women-Boxed Set
King Of Pain Vol.#1
King Of Pain Vol.#2
Shades Of Shay Collection
Cobra's Christmas
Cajun Queens Boxed Set

www.ingramcontent.com/pod-product-compliance
Lightning Source LLC
Chambersburg PA
CBHW021443150726
47989CB00001B/370